LEARNING TO PRAY IN THE AGE OF TECHNIQUE

ALSO BY GONÇALO M. TAVARES
IN ENGLISH TRANSLATION

Jerusalem

LEARNING TO PRAY IN THE AGE OF TECHNIQUE

LENZ BUCHMANN'S POSITION IN THE WORLD

gonçalo m. tavares
translated by daniel hahn

Dalkey Archive Press
Champaign / Dublin / London

Originally published in Portuguese as *Aprender a rezar na Era da Técnica* by Editorial Caminho, SA, 2007
Copyright © Gonçalo M. Tavares, 2007 by arrangement with Literarische Agentur Mertin Inh. Nicole Witt e. K., Frankfurt am Main, Germany
Translation copyright © 2011 by Daniel Hahn
First Edition, 2011

Library of Congress Cataloging-in-Publication Data

Tavares, Gonçalo M., 1970-
[Aprender a rezar na era da Técnica. English]
Learning to pray in the age of technique / Gonçalo M. Tavares ; Translated by Daniel Hahn.
-- 1st ed.
    p. cm.
"Originally published in Portuguese as Aprender a rezar na Era da Técnica by Editorial Caminho, SA, 2007."
ISBN 978-1-56478-627-2 (pbk. : alk. paper)
I. Hahn, Daniel. II. Title.
PQ9282.A89A6713 2011
869.3'5--dc23
                        2011017148

Partially funded by a grant from the Illinois Arts Council, a state agency, and by the University of Illinois at Urbana-Champaign

The publication of this book was partly supported by the DGLB—Direcção-Geral do Livro e das Bibliotecas / Portugal

www.dalkeyarchive.com

Cover: design and composition by Danielle Dutton, illustration by Nicholas Motte
Printed on permanent/durable acid-free paper and bound in the United States of America

PART ONE
STRENGTH

APPRENTICESHIP

1

The adolescent Lenz learns about cruelty

His father grabbed him and took him to the room of one of the servant girls, the youngest and prettiest in the house.

"You're doing her now, here, in front of me."

The servant-girl was scared, of course, but what was strange was that she seemed to be scared of him, not of his father: it was the fact that Lenz was an adolescent that scared the little servant girl, not the violence with which the father treated his son, completely without modesty, without even taking the trouble to leave the room. His father wanted to see it.

"You're doing her in front of me," he repeated.

These words of his father's would mark Lenz for years. 'You're doing her.'

The act of fornicating with the little servant girl was reduced to the simplest of verbs—doing. "You're doing her," that was the expression, as though the servant-girl was not yet fully done, as though she were matter still unshaped, awaiting his action, Lenz's action, to complete her. This woman is not yet made till you've done her, thought Lenz the adolescent, clearly, and his next gestures were those of a worker, an employee following the instructions of another more experienced, in this case his father: you're doing her.

"Take off your trousers." That was the second thing his father said. "Take off your trousers."

The adolescent Lenz took his trousers off. And all the orders that followed were directed exclusively at him—that is to say, his father did not address a single phrase to the servant girl—she knew what had to be done and she did what had to be done, a machine without any choice. Unlike the adolescent Lenz who, in spite of everything, was able to say to his father, "I don't want to."

"Take off your trousers," his father commanded.

And then Lenz was led, almost pushed, by his father, over to the servant girl, lying there, waiting.

"Go ahead," said his father, roughly.

And the adolescent Lenz, determined, went ahead, onto the servant girl.

2

The hunt

Lenz pulls on his boots and prepares for the hunt. First comes the ritual of taking control of the various small, immobile objects: the boots, the gun, the heavy waistcoat.

These were the best movements for contributing to the formation of a human being. And to how a good shot he was.

In turn, the more agile elements of nature insisted on a disobedience Lenz found it impossible to tolerate. He went hunting out of a particular political determination. A rabbit was a tiny adversary, but it obliged Lenz to occupy a particular position on the earth, within a combat zone. This meagre opponent—a rabbit—forced Lenz into tensing his muscles, into mobilizing his cunning: just aiming wasn't enough, the weapon's mechanical capabilities weren't enough, an intellectual attention was needed too, an attention of the intelligence: only immobile things did without this attention of Lenz's.

Between him—Lenz—and the still living quarry, there was a pre-established agreement: he refused to kill a single animal in the first few minutes of the hunt. This was a demand made by the force of habit, a sort of respect shown in relation to the space being invaded. It wasn't Lenz's home.

The twenty minutes when he didn't fire a shot were his way of wiping his feet on the mat of the strange house he was entering. Strangeness existed in the forest, and since there was no front door and no doormat, Lenz spent twenty minutes going down the paths that nature—in its own very particular stupidity—left open, willingly, for men to make their way through.

There was another law in the forest. Morality in the forest was indelicate, crude; it was like going into the bedroom of the little servant girl when he was an adolescent; into that back room, filled with smells so different to those found in the main house, in his parents' house. In the little servant girl's room to be gentle was to be weak, and was such an absurd mistake that even the girl herself protested at any affectionate gesture made by the master's son.

In the forest, virtue hadn't been invaded by the smell of mold; there was another power suspended over him as Lenz walked between the trees, solid trees but twisted, trees which hid hundreds of animal existences within them—existences that were, after all, themselves hunted quarries, in what was also an extraordinarily good synthesis of human relations.

Lenz didn't have any illusions: the only reason he didn't walk the streets of the city with the same caution and with his weapon cocked to fire was because, in that space, there was something that inhibited his hatred: mutual economic advantage.

The apparent equilibrium between neighbors in the same building is something that even a man of high standing experiences right up until the moment when—helpless—he sets foot into the swamp. The expression "After you," spoken by someone in a café to another customer entering at the same time, thus accepting that he will get his drink only after the other has been served—these are words of warfare, of pure warfare. Any words of sympathy can be seen—if looked at another way—as words of attack. By letting the other person go ahead of him, the first man wasn't agreeing to take second place but instead preparing a map of the terrain, the better to keep visual control over his target, who for a few moments believed himself to have won an advantage. The benefit of someone being ahead of us, Lenz's father had once said, is that he has his back to us. It doesn't matter where we are, what matters is field of vision and relative position.

It wasn't long, however, before Lenz understood that some kind of support was necessary, something the body could lean on without fear of being betrayed; a wall, essentially, that ran no risk of collapsing. The family would be his wall, the place where he could rest the back of his neck (for even during a violent attack the attacker himself still has a neck—it's important never to forget this fragility).

Lenz readied his weapon, rested the steel of the butt on his chest—a chest that was pounding hard—and, thinking about the little servant girl whom, more than ten years earlier, under his father's encouragements, he had done for the first time, Lenz took aim and fired.

Then there was a squeal, which in another situation he would have sworn had come from the wheels of a car, and after a moment of being inexplicably stunned, he began to run toward it. Soon the blood had become conspicuous in that part of the forest, yet Lenz still couldn't catch the animal.

He had managed to wound the enemy, but not to eliminate it. He still couldn't eat it.

A COMPLETELY INAPPROPRIATE SONG

1

Let's see what Lenz is up to

Breaking completely with his habits, Lenz decided that night to allow a beggar in.

Lenz was laughing.

"I'll give you your bread."

At Lenz's request his wife brought the day's paper. As she handed it to him, she said, "Please, give him what he wants then send him away."

Lenz gently stroked his wife's backside and laughed at the tramp. He asked her to leave. "Man talk," he said, and he smiled again.

"Have you seen the news?" Lenz asked the tramp, holding out the newspaper face up.

"I'm hungry," said the man.

Lenz didn't reply. He was still holding the newspaper.

"Look at this: the president says that at last the populace is getting a bit of peace and quiet. See? What kind of peace and quiet is this? What do you think?"

"Please . . ." repeated the man.

Lenz continued reading the headlines on the front page: "There's a new class on the rise: businessmen with their money are now taking up political positions and starting to worry about the state of the country rather than worrying exclusively about the state of their factories. Did you hear?" asked Lenz.

"Don't humiliate me," said the man.

Lenz told him not to be ridiculous.

"You should have some respect for the country. You know the anthem? I'm going to give you food. Want some? And money?"

The tramp shifted slightly. He was standing: Lenz still hadn't allowed him to sit down on the small stool that was empty beside him.

"But sing the anthem first," asked Lenz. "At every opportunity . . . Never losing sight of the meaning of existence, you see? Each man's duties, having been born into a certain country; you understand? Do you know the anthem? Might I ask you to sing it? We still have time. The food is on its way. Please go ahead, please, do start."

2
Contracts and sums

After some discussion Lenz tore up the contract when he was exactly half way through his signature. Half of my name, but it'll never reach the end, thought Lenz. My name interrupted, and the deal interrupted. "There's not enough in it for me," said Lenz.

The tension in the room changed as he approached—with the hand that was holding the pen—a mere contract for the purchase of the living-room furniture. Signing his name was a great responsibility. And it wasn't just a question of law, it was more than that.

Lenz's wife was not a woman who gave any thought to what to do beyond the following day. She was a strange woman, who seemed to accept everything with a passivity mingled with a certain perverseness that sometimes ended up annoying even Lenz. She added everything up, one occurrence followed another, and she accepted everything—there was no reflection.

Lenz, on the other hand, didn't consider life simply a sum of actions and occurrences, life also presupposed operations whose power was closer to that of subtraction, multiplication, or division. All the primary algebraic operations existed in daily life, in the private life of each human being.

"Not always a matter of adding up, not always a matter of adding up," Lenz would say, in a tone of utter revulsion, on the day they buried his father, Frederich Buchmann.

Death, for example. Not always a matter of adding up.

3

The brain

A man—Lenz—can size up the decisive points of his body, with his body being the map of a State and the identifying of these points of greatest power the beginnings of a plan of attack.

The decisive points in one's anatomy? In the first place, the head, or more properly the skull, that group of bones that protects the instrument used for perceiving the world. It isn't intelligence, however, nor the extraordinary capacity for abstraction, but the rough and ancient capability to resist the outside world, the material and animal resistance that remain in that intelligence, which it is important to protect. A man who is illiterate, or unable to add three to three, can still consider his head a decisive point as long as he knows how to pick up a weapon and differentiate the blade end from the handle, the barrel from the trigger. The head teems with surprising detours and capabilities—the map of a city where the little alleyways ramify out to infinity— but the most important of all is the main thoroughfare: the brain is there in order to keep us from letting ourselves get killed. It demands that our enemies be extremely skillful. "Let's not complicate things," Lenz thought to himself. "The brain, when seen up close, and understood thoroughly, has the form and function of a weapon, no more than that."

4

Asking for more bread

"She's a fine woman—you see?"

At last the man is sitting on a stool in the kitchen, he's already eating something and now he's sipping at some soup, noisily.

Lenz lifts his wife's skirt, turns her rump toward the tramp, pushes her against the sink, drops his trousers, pulls down her panties (she helps), pulls out his penis, and quickly penetrates her.

The couple is three meters from the tramp, who barely raises his eyes toward them, afraid to look. Lenz fornicates furiously with his wife, and she allows herself to be taken completely, she accepts everything; the tramp is facing Lenz's naked, heaving buttocks.

The man seems to say something, to himself, addressing no one else; he murmurs something, something imperceptible.

There is some food over to his right, but the man doesn't get up; he decides to wait till the couple stops. Without any haste, without looking up from the table, in an orderly manner; he had time, he thought.

THE DOCTOR IN THE AGE OF TECHNIQUE

1
The hand that holds the scalpel

Dr. Lenz is received by two helpful nurses at the entrance to the operating theater. The doctor in Age of Technique is looked upon as though he was a skilful driver. The car waits serenely for the arrival of its owner—just like a pet dog, except that machines don't entertain themselves or sink into existential crises when their boss isn't around. Nothing of the sort, not at either extreme: machinery understands neither the playful nor the tragic, it understands direction, a certain force, a certain movement. A movement that is, as it were, intellectual, and deliberate—there is nothing in a machine that is as stupid as a dog who, with no sense of timing, salivates when there's no food anywhere in sight, just because it's ill, or as an animal who limps and even having only three available legs tries to attack or run away. Machines are far more sensible.

Lenz is a surgeon, Dr. Lenz B., his skill contained, concentrated in his right hand which, well supported by a left hand that plays the role of specialist observer, didn't take many years to earn its reputation. His right hand has an aura, an unscientific glimmer about it: an extra finger, as it were, an invisible finger whose touch—that final touch—can, in extreme cases, save. Dr. Lenz B. has already saved many men and many women.

In his right hand the scalpel gleams; there is a certain something extra about the combination of this medical instrument with Lenz's hand that provokes those in attendance at any operation to keep their eyes fixed only on the area immediately surrounding them. In a situation of extreme cold, that hand, holding the scalpel, would be fire.

Some have even likened the spectacle to sessions of hypnosis: the absolute, convincing slowness of Lenz's right hand transformed into a fairground hypnotist: all the attendant nurses and the younger doctors focus their worthier instincts of observation and hold their breaths, as though watching the climax of a film. Lenz's wrist holds steady as though supported by a length of metal rather than an arm. All that moves are the fingers; the scalpel an instrument able to affect us far more deeply than a musical instrument: whatever feelings of tragedy or celebration are born from this instrument are acute in the extreme. Precise and profound, this right hand, with its scalpel, expressed the various degrees of intensity one could have, in the world: here, music really could kill or save. The scalpel came into contact with the body and went right into it, it didn't circle it, or edge around it.

"We're not dealing with feelings here," Lenz said once, "we're dealing with veins and arteries, with vessels that have broken and which we must repair, with swellings that release substances that seem—though they have come from within—that seem nonetheless to be alien to the body."

Inside a body the scalpel sought to reinstate lost order. It brought back laws: knowing the cause, the effects could be guessed at; it was a matter—and Lenz would sometimes say this—of install-ing a new monarchy; the scalpel proclaimed a new Kingdom: it restored the organism's roads, straightened up whatever ruins needed straightening up, or, on the contrary, knocked down once and for all anything that was still standing but that had lost its foundations, and through this knocking down constructed a new horizontal plane; if everything had been knocked down and noth-ing could be raised up again, then we would come to accept this new state of being: "We would lie down, and observe," said Lenz.

In turn, illness was clearly a form of cellular anarchy, a disor-der, an internal disrespect for the rules that some people even call divine, as they preceded any human arrangement. A body is not a city. There may have been a pre-existing map, but hu-mans were not given the privilege of examining it and suggest-ing amendments.

Of course, a new world was beginning now. A more power-ful action would bring the Gods down; the gleam of things was already the *only* gleam in things, a bonfire cast light thanks to its concrete matter alone, the divine was no longer an element *that illuminates even further*, it was simply another thing, beyond the opposition between dark and light. Electricity, Lenz used to say, had made certain assumptions about the divine ridiculous. It is impossible to feel fear and respect toward something that could be mistaken for nothing more than a powerful electrical discharge.

2

Explosion and precision

The most amazing thing about Lenz's operations was that at a certain moment the scalpel, and even his right hand, seemed to dissolve into the body of the patient being operated on. The scalpel entered the body like a dagger, and seemed to be seeking something far more amazing than just a particular artery; the scalpel marked the first point of attack; an attack that, in this case, aimed to save the one being attacked.

Lenz occasionally had a feeling that was almost magical, soberly irrational—he saw his scalpel as searching not for some poorly functioning artery or vessel but for something less material, more (the word does apply) spiritual. As though his scalpel could even detect the patient's individual guilt, a guilt that wasn't necessarily moral but which was certainly organic. A sick organism seemed to Lenz materially guilty; he had constructed, in his mind, a morality of tissues, a morality composed of black cells or white cells, burned cells or intact ones, and in this context immorality was simply a failure to function.

In not many years' practice Lenz had learned that, in medicine, two opposing, equally astonishing technical forces were opposed and struggling for dominance: explosion and precision. The two extremes were each other's adversaries. His scalpel, it was quite clear, was the messenger of precision and rightness. The sick organism, or a part of it, had blundered down a cul-de-sac, and with its strength the scalpel would provide material aid in reminding it which was the correct track, which the main road.

Which was why Lenz always found it strange when surgical interventions were the result of an explosion—as had happened in a factory some months earlier. A machine whose insides were in a state of disorder had exploded and this had provoked a similar state of disorder on the insides of an individual. Lenz had managed to save the man's life, and during the operation had felt with unusual intensity the struggle between the two extremes of medical technique: his scalpel embodying precision, morality, the legality that this facet of technique both establishes and requires, and, on the other hand, on the sick man's side, there were the clear results of an explosion likewise provoked by technique; the explosion that instantly establishes disorder—whether on a large scale (a battlefield of soldiers) or a personal one—and cellular panic, which is simply the temporary establishment of a marked immorality: there isn't a single straight line left in a body that has just experienced the effects of an explosion. A bomb, deep down, from a schematic point of view—just like a photocopier is a machine designed to produce photocopies—is simply a machine designed to explode.

Lenz's scalpel was therefore the material voice of human ethics, and a bomb the material voice of perversion and the deregulation of habits. However, the two opposing sides were made of exactly the same substance. They were sons, not of the same God, but of the same man, which Lenz found fascinating.

And just as he found these two worlds fascinating, Lenz never forgot, when he was operating on someone, that the slightest diversion of his scalpel, through accident or error, could lead to the death of the organism being operated upon.

When his right hand—exact and magical—was acting, the decision to go left or to go right was not simply a question of traffic, it didn't mean progressing via a shorter or longer route. It was, rather, a matter of living or not living, of remaining alive or not. It wasn't the length of the journey, the time that this or that path took. A wrong decision on the scalpel's part—turning left when you ought to have turned right—wasn't equivalent to some minor annoyance provoked by a delay due to a poor choice while navigating the space of the city. No, a diversion of a few millimeters on the part of his right hand could take a body to one of two opposing worlds: the world of a living body—albeit a sick one, or one with its capabilities diminished—or the world of a corpse, which is something else entirely.

As he steered his scalpel, Lenz saw the operation as he might see a stereo—something that could be turned off or kept on, depending on his decision. To the right—always to the right, a straight line, the side where the Lord (Lenz joked) had placed moral men—moving to the right kept the human system switched on, while turning left—the side of the devil or of the movements that we do not understand—turned off the system, cut off the electricity. And it was Lenz who was in charge of the crucial switch.

3

Competence is not determined by the heart

Up to that point he had always gone the right way, but each time he took up his scalpel for another operation Dr. Lenz Buchmann couldn't stop himself thinking about that other possibility, which yet again he had available to him: he could turn the switch in the wrong direction, deliberately switching the mechanism off. And however much it shocked him—as his profession was the one moral stronghold he still maintained in a life he knew to be utterly disordered—in spite of this, Lenz always felt attracted to the second possibility, to the negative path he would never choose to take.

Yes, his profession would always be protected from his unvarying refusal to have any truck with virtue: he was alive, he was strong and rich; he only toyed with virtue out of playfulness, for pleasure, never out of necessity. When he operated, however, he was transformed into a respecter of the laws of the city and of all generally-held convictions about good and evil. He accepted them just like a soldier, an animal that had learned its lesson well. And that was why he saved the sick men he operated on: his scalpel fought against the forces of explosion and re-established precision and order. He felt worthy because his right hand was "in combat" (when he operated), and his hand was worthy too. But with each day that passed, the praise and the admiration of technique that his patients, his medical colleagues, and the hospital staff directed at him became intolerable. He didn't mind being considered competent, but that this competence should be confused with a sort of goodness—a sentiment he utterly despised—was unacceptable. And their confusion—unable to see the difference between goodness and technical competence—began to erode the barrier Lenz had built between his profession and his private life, in which the total dissolution of moral values was absolutely obvious. The pleasure he took in humiliating prostitutes, weak women, adolescents, beggars who knocked on his door, even his own wife, couldn't stand in starker contrast to the holy aura with which some of the relatives of the sick people he'd operated on had surrounded him. This was why, on that afternoon, when that ingenuous woman, thanking him for having operated successfully on her mother, said to him,

"You're a good man!"

he felt the need (right there in front of the hospital staff) to reply, roughly,

"Sorry, I'm nothing of the sort. I'm a doctor."

AN EXPLOSION

1

The intoxication of survivors

The intoxication prompted by an explosion is of such an intensity that it makes all other forms of intoxication, from all other sources, seem trifles. First of all, when a bomb goes off, the delusion, the abrupt diversion of rationality to a state of emergency requiring a different sort of rationality, is collective and not individual. At the same time, the inexplicable feeling that links all the people in the vicinity of an explosion, after a bomb blows up . . . fear and the practical need for certain actions are not enough to explain it.

There is actually the sense that—from one moment to the next— the bystanders have indeed ingested some toxic substance, a substance perhaps created by the shock and the surprise of the explosion, but which remains in the seconds that follow. Therefore, its effects are not reducible to a single moment. This substance that intoxicates and obliges people to act like some other kind of animal, it seems uncontrollable, and no specialist—no psychologist specializing in behavior at times of crisis—could ever predict the doses in which it comes to be distributed in different organisms.

2
Movement and immobility. Attack and defense.

Within that landscape—previously calm, rational, and ordered—the bomb exploded amid a number of soldiers who were carrying out subsidiary tasks. It was as if the devil himself had dropped into that landscape—or a plane, out of control—and, in falling, at the moment of impact, this everyday devil haphazardly scattered red sparks across the ground.

Countless soldiers had been hit. It was an assassination attempt on an important officer, but it was still that officer who, following the explosion, continued to be the one to give the orders.

This officer still had a core of the old authority in him, of the law that preceded the catastrophe, which allowed the others to feel just a tiny bit of security. They could believe that there wasn't any more danger only because the tide of blood hadn't risen to the point where it interrupted the voice of command. A boat sinking under the certain, incontestable orders of its captain is a boat that—in spite of everything—is going down in an organized and human fashion; just like a man who, before committing suicide, leaves his home clean and tidy, puts on his best suit, and carefully cleans the rust off the gun, to be sure that nothing will go wrong.

There was, however, general turmoil in the city. Ambulances circulated at triumphant speeds—and this statement of their usefulness elevated all the unmade bodies and the repeating calls for help onto another plane.

Naturally, Dr. Lenz was called to the hospital. The hammer had struck a blow, and men were needed who knew how to reverse the effects of the metal already dissolving into some of the victims' bodies. The bombs had left pieces of itself in nearby organisms, turning the doctors into hurried fishermen, retrieving the bits of refuse that someone had deliberately introduced into a system which was so tranquil that it might otherwise have allowed itself to slip into tedium. Lenz, however, stuck to his theory, a theory that he was always trying to corroborate: an inactive man, struck by a bullet traveling at the same speed and in the same conditions as another man who was, by contrast, in combat, alert, with his energies focused, would die much more quickly. The bored man would die in an instant; the man on the move and alert might yet survive. More than this, Lenz distinguished between two kinds of motion: attack and defense. An attack makes the organism perpetrating it not immortal but at least closer to being so. And in that sense, there was, for Lenz, a hierarchy, not only of strength but of resistance to bullets: the strongest and, so to speak, most immortal were those moving, attacking, followed by those moving defensively, and then, last, the most fragile, the most mortal—in short, the sickest: those who do not move, those who are bored.

But Dr. Lenz had to suspend his daydreaming: there were already some men arriving whom this swift and malevolent technique had struck down as they advanced. So they deserved to be saved.

3

Please withdraw, this room is not for you

The art of finding metal shards in the middle of a body—his right hand wandered through that space, albeit in a particular direction, a destination in sight.

The only reason Lenz didn't burst out laughing was because he wasn't alone; his movements—which seemed hidden now inside a second glove, the body of the injured soldier—were mockeries of themselves. Lenz felt as though he was engaged in a kind of manual labor that for him, deep down, was like manipulating shapes in clay or working a piece of wood. Any feelings of empathy were dissolved in professional expertise and in the recognition of his triumph in relation to the body lying on the stretcher. Lenz was alive, on his feet, with his reason intact, and still in control of the use of language: in that room he was the person who determined every Yes and every No—and he had long known that controlling such extreme words was a source of undisputable power.

A startled nurse was asking Dr. Lenz whether he wanted her to pass him another scalpel, one with a fine point, and Lenz replied: "No. No, no. Yes, yes, yes."

Let us say that "organic craftsmanship," the most basic crafts-manship, often filled him with enthusiasm. Lenz knew that bullets or bomb shrapnel—in short, all the pieces of metal that find their way into our bodies—were only looking for what any living creature looks for: a shelter, a final home, a home where they can be left alone, where they feel secure. And what might seem like a search for shelter to one individual might also seem, to outside observers, like flight: something or someone trying to hide. Lenz knew it was essential to root out such pieces of metal before each bit found its final home, because then, however great his ability, it would be very difficult to extract—not the piece of metal itself, but its effects on the structure of the nearby organs and cells Lenz was so familiar with. Ultimately, though, it was true: metal, however small a piece it might be, has just the same instinct as a hare, or any other animal in the forest trying to escape the eyes of the hunter and find some indestructible shelter. And what was at stake in the speed of his scalpel was the conflict between this shelter, the comfort and security the metal might find, and the life of the man who had been hit. The danger to the man's vitality was the sheltering—the bourgeoisification, Lenz would have said—of the metal, and its effects on that final hiding place, that final cubic millimeter of the body.

The commotion, meanwhile, grew and diminished, the hospital wards seeming to obey the same laws as the tides. Meanwhile, the concentration of rationality there decreased in inverse proportion to the arrival of more bloodied bodies; the sight of the bodies' sudden incoherence, while only physical, seemed to affect every unit of the great weapon of collective humanity: the calculated and developed way decisions are made. Some of the nurses bumped into one another, two doctors gave contradictory instructions for handling the same injury; in short, there was in some people there an evident illiteracy when it came to discussing what had happened, which was not far short of a catastrophe. Many of the people in the hospital were barely ready to deal with normality—and normality now seemed to be just another name for eternity: a repetition to infinity of a given sequence of events.

Now he was shouting at a nurse who was shaking as though each of the injured men was her lover, her father or son. She was seized by such an attack of nerves that it made her forget everything she'd learned; she mixed up all her intended movements.

So after one more clumsy motion, Lenz shouted at the nurse: "No!" and with a rough gesture pointed her out of the room.

"If you don't know how to pick up a scalpel or to handle the machines properly," he said, "get out of this room. Get out!" he actually shouted.

He had no need for her, for her irrationality.

Let her go pray outside. Not here, here was something else.

And the nurse had to leave the room.

A RETURN TO CALM

1

Able to hate nature, able to be hated by her

"Yes," replied Lenz, without looking up, to the offer of a cigarette.

The state of things had changed and the uproar was over. The weapons that events seemed to have pointed at Lenz's head, saying "Act!", had been lowered. Dr. Lenz B. could smoke a cigarette without worrying.

"The storm has passed," someone said, but the truth was that it hadn't been a storm but a lack of synchrony between the organic fragility of the soldiers and an activity perhaps more extreme than the way most humans tend to pass their time. Deep down, a catastrophe is an excessive demand for action on the part of the events: human beings just aren't capable of accomplishing so many things in such a short span of time. Everything that is very fast—or even instantaneous—is stronger than man; and strength, therefore, is really a synonym for speed. In natural cataclysms, too, the elements involved are simply quicker on the draw.

Lenz had no illusions about the earth on which he walked: between nature and man there was a breaking point that had been exceeded long ago. There was a new light in the cities, the technical light, a light that produced substantive transformations that no animal had ever achieved before; and this new brightness only increased the hatred that the most ancient elements in the world seemed always to have harbored for man. Lenz was just as frightened of an earthquake as he was afraid of a sunny day during which unknown birds seemed to be beginning an eternal friendship with pairs of lovers who hadn't met each other yet. On those peaceful days, Lenz saw a healthiness that was fake, a preparation for cruelty—someone was carefully cleaning the gallows the night before the victim was due to set foot on it. He felt no excitement at the order of the elements—he knew full well that it was a system that had nothing to do with the order of the cities, where conductors, laws, and policemen point the way for the proper progression of music and criminals. But all the things that nature found to be orderly were alien to the city.

Sometimes Lenz went so far as to formulate the question—steering his mind toward some peaceful garden—"What's it thinking about?" as though he and nature were engaged in a contest where rationality was key (though strength of muscle and strength of will all mattered too, of course). To Lenz, a peaceful day was just a day when nature was healthy, and in that sense a day when she was gathering the strength that sooner or later she would use to launch an attack against humanity. Lenz did not trust nature.

They—that is, men and the elements of nature—were, deep down, simply things that had been put in the same space, but which did not share a single historical moment. Nature had no history, actually—everything repeated itself; the concrete elements of a landscape that still hadn't seen the wheel, that still was traveled over by carts, while men had long ago built high-speed airplanes. Really, the history of nature was still at its starting point, it hadn't even begun yet, the second day had not yet dawned, it was still the first morning; *nature hasn't even invented fire yet*, Lenz used to say, repeating an idea of his father's, Frederich Buchmann.

There wasn't a single historical difference between the wind that he could now feel blowing though a hospital window and the wind that had touched the face of a Roman emperor. And that immutability wasn't a symptom of weakness. On the contrary, its impermeability to history, to the changing conditions of things, that was nature's major weapon, and in that sense this was where its danger lay: the end that burned. Meanwhile, if materials and the ways of transforming them by means of those useful methodologies of torture—twisting, dissolving, fusing—had indeed evolved, human passions had nonetheless been immobilized. Not a single new feeling had appeared in Lenz's generation. Contrary to what the Bible says, new things do exist under the sun, but what doesn't exist is anything new under the skin. The heart fights the same battles and faces the same decisions as hearts of old. Yes, new techniques and new medicines (of which Lenz was a faithful representative) did of course allow the *prolonging* of the passions; but for Lenz this only meant that human beings were now able to hate till later.

To prolong one's lifespan, that most existential of questions, was—Lenz believed—merely to provide an additional period for the incubation of hatred, for the incubation of the battles and disjunctions between the opinions, aims, and customs of various human beings. It was quite clear to Lenz, each time he saved a person's life by way of some surgical procedure, that he was saving only one man—a statistical nonentity. Statistics are a precise way of demonstrating indifference.

2
What does a finger matter?

Looking at a chart of population statistics, with its successive columns of numbers, had always been an experience that allowed Lenz to understand each of the actions perpetrated by the most violent of regimes. The numbers made up a negative intensity that completely cancelled out any proximity of two individual bodies.

As he held a chart that showed the number of doctors and hospital employees distributed by section, a chart without any names, showing only the *quantity* for each medical specialization and operating theatre, as he held this "document," Lenz sometimes amused himself by asking his colleagues—as he pointed to the numbers in the table—where they were.

And some of them, the more naïve among them, went along with it, and tried—using ordinary logic—to locate their position, their place in that heap of digits. Deep down they were trying to transform a number into a name, and their efforts to find the column and row in the chart to which they belonged was received by Lenz with a cynical smile of sympathy: he seemed to be listening to the pleas of a man condemned to the gas chamber, begging not to be next. The question was too serious, however: if you don't want to be next, tell me who should go in your place. Give me a name to replace yours. Lenz knew it was this tragic cynicism that could synthesize humanity. Tell me who should go in your place.

But the world didn't stop moving, and Dr. Lenz Buchmann was interrupted in the middle of his reflections and the cigarette he was smoking by a small commotion: a civilian who'd suffered a small work accident (and so nothing to do with the explosion) and who had lost his right index finger, was disturbing the hospital's silence with his persistent yells. He was trying to get the attention of a nurse and insisted on getting out of bed. He was there, this little man, right there in the corridor, when Lenz approached him to reprimand him:

"What's your name?"

"Joseph Walser."

"Well then, Mr. Joseph Walser, please behave yourself."

The little man was quite evidently embarrassed, and Dr. Lenz turned his back on him. What does a finger matter? Just a coward, he thought.

THE BROTHER

1

Something calling from the other side

Lenz consults the patients' files. The letter A. Then the letter B. Albert. Albert Buchmann.

The files place their subjects' heads one next to another, in a sequence of technical decapitations—false, but nonetheless striking; showing X-ray and CAT-scan images of their skulls opposite each name. All the heads looked just the same on the inside as on the outside, but of course the images didn't show intellectual differences: the skull of a fool without even a grasp of language is no different from the skull of a student or a man of action.

Lenz was fascinated by this "neutral stupidity" of the skeleton, this objective crudeness of the X-ray, creating an invisible democracy whose connotations bore little resemblance to the feelings triggered by a normal picture—a photograph, say.

Each one of those skulls would surely have a distinctive face, capable of attracting or repelling him. Certain faces were immediate declarations of war, while others, on the contrary, were so weak, their expressions so compromised by the external world, that a man with any pride would refuse to have them even as his servants. Daring, the capacity for self-denial, the intensity made available for sacrifice or for comfort, all these were qualities or defects belonging to the world of the facial expression, yet what Lenz was now observing was the world of the indeterminate, the shapeless, the face of the species and not of the individual. He was, in short, observing the bones of the head, those constructs of ancient engineering that allow heads to rise up to accept a duel, or lower to avoid looking at someone who is suffering. There was no happiness or unhappiness in those skulls; some simply presented black stains that didn't belong to the world of safety or of health, but rather to the world of death, of a death that is as yet incomplete (that is, illness), but already approaching with great strides.

He looked at the skull of Albert, his brother: two enormous black marks.

There was something that was beginning to require the presence of Albert Buchmann in some other place.

2

X-ray and landscape

What had always fascinated Lenz about illness was the uselessness of work—a sick man couldn't work to make himself better. And in that sense man's great capacity was stolen from him: the capacity to build, the capacity simply to make. *To make* was the great human verb, clearly separating man from the ant, the dog, the plants: his *makings* were gigantic, powerful; never quite immortal but far more permanent than anything else constructed by any other species.

This *making* was what made man worthy of a great enemy, a new enemy, yet to appear, now that all the animal species had long ago lowered their guard and been conquered. It had in fact been this *making* that destroyed the bonds which used to link man to the landscape.

Just like with those stripped skulls: you could only see the landscape when the face of the world lost its flesh. And its new flesh, the new face of the landscape, was a human face, placed everywhere. The skull of the natural elements was covered now by billions of human beings, in addition to bridges, factories, tall buildings competing with one another in a motionless cockfight (who can rise higher, who can house more people).

Lenz felt that man lacked the science to X-ray the elements of the natural world. *To look at the skull of the landscape*, that's the aim, Lenz muttered to himself as he closed the drawer on his files, still holding in his right hand the X-ray of the skull of Albert Buchmann, his brother, who quite clearly didn't have more than a year left to live. Two stains of black greed had settled themselves in a place from which they would never depart: they had found their place of final shelter in his brother's head.

And how did Lenz feel about this? The death foretold of Albert Buchmann, his older brother? Nothing: absolutely nothing. He looked at that X-ray as though at a landscape. He turned his back on it in just the same way.

X-RAY AND DESIRE

1

Ritual and adjustment

A spontaneous—and at first almost playful—provocation began to transform itself into a habit, dependent now on the forces that surround desire: that tramp returned to the house of Dr. Lenz B.—got his bread, ate, received money—and Dr. Lenz would repeat what his wife accepted, passively, almost gladly, as a new commitment arranged between herself and her husband. In front of the tramp, in the kitchen, Lenz fornicated with her. His wife—Maria Buchmann—accepted everything, with the refinement gained from occasionally pretending to be naïve, surprised—she who was the very opposite of all that.

But first the tramp had to be humiliated with an unusual slowness. Lenz—or even his wife—moved as if to fetch some money from his wallet to give the man, but then stopped and said: "It's not time yet."

Lenz would read and comment on the news in the day's papers, he would ask him questions, mock the man's ignorance: *Where have you been all this time? You're so badly informed. Aren't you interested in politics?*

And the ritual was upheld for each visit: Lenz wouldn't give him any money or food until the tramp had sung the national anthem. The first few times Lenz would correct lines that had become corrupted, but now the tramp could sing it correctly, without any mistakes.

One night, when he had not yet called his wife over to join them—deliberately increasing her excitement through anticipation—Dr. Lenz said, all of a sudden, to this man whose name he'd never asked in six months:

"You know my brother Albert is going to die? He's got two marks here—" he pointed, "—in his head."

2
Measuring the evil

In his right hand Lenz holds the X-ray of the skull of his brother Albert B., and shows it to this man who—as always—hardly says a word, nodding his head, trying to listen, showing that he is alert.

"Here, look," and Lenz points at the two smudges on the X-ray.

The two of them are sitting at the kitchen table. The tramp has only eaten a bread roll. There's food on the table, but Lenz has not yet allowed the man to help himself. The tramp is trying to forget his appetite and to concentrate on his conversation with Lenz, because he knows that if he doesn't show interest it will get worse: Dr. Lenz will prolong the ritual still further and might even become irritated, send him away without food and without money. The key is his facial expression, and above all the look in his eyes: the tramp knows it's the eyes that can ruin everything. Which is why he struggles to focus a certain energy, the energy of attentiveness around his eyes. And this sense of attentiveness aimed at a particular target was a singular and indivisible unit: it wasn't possible to be attentive simultaneously to the smell of the food and to the X-ray of the skull that Dr. Lenz was showing him. The tramp's efforts were impressive. He already knew the rules of the game, and there was just one object: to receive money or eat, that was all. And to achieve that, he knew what he had to do. And right now it was this: to demonstrate his interest in this X-ray of a head.

"Look," Lenz insists, "two smudges, huge." Lenz pointed at the smudges. "I'll go get a ruler and measure them."

Dr. Lenz gets up, leaves the kitchen, goes into the house. The tramp stays where he is, sitting; he tries not to move, tries not even to look at the food. His stomach still aches, but he must wait.

Dr. Lenz returns. He is carrying a ruler.

"Found it. A ruler. You practically need a map to find a ruler in this place. You know my wife . . ." Lenz laughs.

The tramp nods.

"Look," says Lenz, holding the ruler and measuring. "One centimeter here, more than a centimeter. And just three millimeters here, but that's a lot. Three millimeters is a lot, so a centimeter is an amount that no one could possibly remove: it's a weight, you see? These things have weight; and at a certain point it's impossible to lift that weight, to take it out of there, out of its place. Medicine doesn't have a crane at its disposal. It really is a question of engineering, but engineering hasn't evolved as quickly in the realm of little things as it has in the realm of large things. Minuscule bugs still cause more trouble than bison; we still haven't found the right caliper for them, you see?"

3
Cinema

"But you know something?" Dr. Lenz went on. "This could as easily be an X-ray of your head as my brother Albert's—there's not a lot of difference. They are two heads: one, two. Of course, in your case, if you had a head like this you wouldn't even have the pleasure of seeing this image: you'd just get bad headaches and then, afterward, not long afterward, it would all be over.

"At least some people get the opportunity to enjoy this sort of movie, a movie unfolding in their own heads. It's almost an entertainment, like any other. But needless to say, the show ends badly. You know what? I'm going to get you some food. Do you want money?"

REFLECTIONS ON ILLNESS

1

Black flower

Sometimes Lenz looks at illness and sees a chance encounter with a passerby who, after knocking into us abruptly, leaves in our hands—distracted—a black flower. But when we try to go return it, the passerby, in haste, has vanished. We begin to run with the black flower in our hand—it doesn't belong to us, the person who lost it might need it—but there's nothing, no trace: the strange passerby has disappeared, evaporated. And in our hands, the black flower. The decision that follows might seem more like a non-decision—a vacillation—but soon our discomfort will stop being a minor detail and become the essential point: ridding ourselves of that repellent flower becomes an urgent necessity. Well then, we're just a few centimeters from a public trash bin, we lift the lid and open our right hand to drop the flower. But something happens: the black flower doesn't leave our hand, it's stuck there, it can't be expelled, *not unless you let your arm go too.* The following days will see countless attempts to—in the first instance—get rid of the black flower, and then to forget about it. At a certain point, however, over the course of a single instant, there will be a change in the organism, similar to changes in a country's currency, in combat with other values, other points of reference; and the man resigns himself to it. No longer is there a black flower; and doctors have a sensible, ancient name for this conjunction of unrealistic facts: illness.

2

A strategy of evil

And what Lenz found most amazing in his trajectory as a doctor was his rapid realization that every illness establishes its own particular science, with its own methodology, its own particular instruments—its unmistakable period of growth and maturation, and its own results, which are always something amazing, something new. It seemed obvious to Lenz that there was someone carrying out experiments on humanity; just like a chemist manipulates substances on his workbench, there was someone combining elements, testing out reactions, introducing slight variations. Illnesses—and that one illness in particular—seek out the best paths, like any living animal, the ones most inclined to movement; and this illness has a logic of infiltration to it. It isn't an abrupt, black, brutal mass that makes something collapse—it isn't a bomb. On the contrary, it seems to take pleasure in not knocking us down right away, allowing us a sinister freedom of movement, a rhythm of suffering per minute or square centimeter, which at first it tries not to exceed, as though its pleasure increases the more its host organism resists. It is an illness whose trajectory takes it along little alleyways; it might begin from a single central point, but quickly scatters to other, insignificant places around the organism. This illness only begins to demand the organism's attention precisely when the latter is about to forfeit the battle. There isn't, then, a body-to-body confrontation; the illness isn't a body, it's a substance that is barely visible, almost transparent; the illness can't be thrown to the floor as one might throw down a man.

Having escaped such a duel, insisting on a subtle guerrilla war, the illness acts through a strategy of successively conquering the organism's allies, and what the various analyses performed over time demonstrated was that various healthy parts of the organism would change sides—month by month—passing over to the other team, to the enemy camp: a yielding that was a combination of surrender and betrayal.

Looking—stunned—at the speed with which the illness progressed in certain individuals, at the incredible surrender of weapons on the part of organs that months earlier had seemed vigorous and unconquerable, Lenz felt that these organs, now tamed by the evil, weren't merely prisoners—because prisoners don't shoot at their old barracks. They were more than this, by now, they were a part of the enemy army; hence the speed with which, after a certain point, death would come to take you. So there was no balance between the world of the living and the world of death. On the one hand there was nothing that could be done, there was no capacity for construction, and on the other, things were indeed done—they were made: there was, obviously, a substance to annihilation, to extinction, to destruction.

3

Two sides, and not one

Nonetheless, the substance in question was—deep down—the same: illness kills by using the same cells that contained all one's great wishes, decisions, and actions of the past: it's all the same matter, but organized differently, now carrying a negative charge.

Man tries to resist, to survive, finding allies in other men and in centuries of medical and technical development, while on the other hand there is illness, likewise strengthened by centuries of its own particular history, a history to which men have no access, but which undoubtedly has its own course, its own highs and lows, its own reversals, revolts, ruins, grandeurs. Illnesses—the emissaries of death—have not stayed still.

There are two organized systems in the world, then, not just one. There is the system of the living, dominated by the great men of the most evolved cities; and then the system of death, perfectly unknown, whose pulleys are of a quite different nature, with its own specific objectives and methods.

The system of death—or, to put it more concretely, the will to death—advanced by a number of means, some of them surprising, but illnesses, and that one illness in particular, were its trump cards. Precisely because they were born from what we would characterize as accidental, unintentional, random. Yet illness isn't the consequence of nature's being distracted. Quite the contrary— nature, thought Lenz (taking this to be everything that is not man, or which is not completely dominated by man) exercises, through illness, a will for combat; an ill will, if considered from a human point of view, or simply a strong will, if the point of view is a neutral, extra-human one.

And it was at this very point, from up high, as high as the mountains, that Lenz would sometimes try to see things: an extra-human looking at the struggle between two forces and two wills, and in the role of spectator marveling at the aesthetics of those sparks, the injured men; refusing to take sides, neither an affective side nor a moral one.

As a doctor, he did of course have an obligation—a professional one, and also on a practical, instrumental level—to position himself and to act on behalf of one side, the human side. But he was merely a soldier in the army that had founded the cities, no more than that: no one would ever hear him cry out for the cause of humanity, he would never suffer for his species just as he would never suffer for his scalpel if it broke accidentally. His way of approaching suffering was as an individual; he did not accept suffering that had been borrowed from others; compassion was an unnecessary feeling, or— as Lenz himself referred to it—*a tool that serves no useful purpose in one's existence*: resolving nothing at all, in technical terms: like someone taking up a hammer to suture two tissues together.

4

Coming to the mountain

As a master of that language which never raises its head, that minuscule language situated between his two hands and the sick cells, Lenz was—above all—someone who loved fresh air, air far removed from the smell and the temperature of the protective machines that a hospital contained in such profusion.

In contact with those silent elements in the world that were not yet controlled by man, Lenz felt close to the real instruments of attack, not those of defense, as in the hospital. In the mountains, in the forests, beside the disordered fields of earth, Lenz felt the thrill of a closeness to something that does not merely want to sustain itself, and whose fight for survival does not require the support of any medical technology.

The earth's disorder was not a scalpel, but a dagger. Alone, wandering through strange places with no trace of metal anywhere near, Lenz truly felt himself to be a soldier from another land, who, having got lost, finds himself in the middle of an army that speaks another language and which advances in attack formation toward his city. And, as this soldier, Lenz knew that the most sensible thing was to do exactly as this foreign army is doing, to try and remain there in the middle of that current of excitement: he doesn't know if he's among the winners, but he is certain that he's with those who are on the attack. And it's there that Lenz Buchmann wants to be.

AN EPISODE WITH A TERMINALLY ILL PATIENT

1

The request

An episode, which ought to be correctly interpreted.

Lenz received a sealed letter from a terminally ill patient, a woman who had been kept in his part of the hospital for many long months.

"It's for my children. It already has the address on it."

Without a doubt it was a request for her children to come see her.

Although he was a man who of course knew all about physical resistance, it was evident that her struggle was coming to an end. Her appearance was already beginning to approach that borderline that turns other people's compassion into a certain amount of disgust, which, even when it's kept in check and humanely reconstructed within the constraints of good behavior, will no longer allow certain spontaneous gestures of assistance or closeness. She had realized this, which was why she had yielded. She—who had never wanted to call for her children— had finally written the letter in which she surrendered, and where no doubt she had said something like *I need to say my good-byes to you.*

Her children—Lenz wasn't sure if there were two or three of them—didn't live in this country. They knew their mother was sick, but considered it to be just a passing malady, something straightforward, not the epilogue to her entire journey.

Lenz took the letter with a gesture of very little intensity, plucking at it with his fingers, a gesture that was almost instinctive, as instinctive as it had been when the woman had sealed the envelope with her saliva, right in front of him, with a movement Lenz felt was utterly inelegant.

He put the envelope in his jacket pocket:

"I'll put it in the post today."

"Yes," said the woman. "Thank you."

Lenz said good-bye, tilting his head slightly, and turned the doorknob.

"I need to say good-bye to them," the woman went on.

"Don't worry," Dr. Lenz replied.

2

The letter

When he arrived home, at the end of that day, after yet another series of requests and minor occurrences, Dr. Lenz removed his jacket and thoughtlessly set down the letter—which was for him already just *a letter* existing among other letters. He put it down on the table where he always put the bits of paper he brought home from the hospital, bits of paper that soon became mixed up with bits of paper from the previous days and yesterday's newspaper.

The following week passed with its usual speed and Dr. Lenz spent little time at home. A few surgical procedures, three of them of great importance, operations to cheat death at the eleventh hour (as Lenz referred to them)—he did nothing that week but maintain the same system of procedures which his activities regularly demanded.

And so the letter from the dying woman spent the week in a pile of other letters and papers. On Saturday, when he had a little time, Lenz stopped to look at his overdue correspondence, opened the letters that were addressed to him, even replying to one that requested his thoughts on some change to the structure of the hospital's auxiliary staff, and then, with no surprise at all, came across the woman's letter. He separated it from his things, placing it now on top of a little stand on the living-room cupboard, for taking out to post later. Now the letter from the dying woman was apart from the other papers, away from the confusion, and perfectly visible in a place in the house he was constantly passing.

3
Everyone has the right to say good-bye

But the days went by, and Lenz forgot all about the letter. Quite unintentionally.

It was just that he worked on a double circuit: one on the outside, made up of his actions and his conversations, and another, inside, invisible and indivisible, which was ultimately the more relevant of the two. This circuit of thoughts occupied him to such a degree that sometimes his own wife had to signal her presence, forcing herself to interfere with her husband's material space, touching him or even pushing him, only gently, so that Lenz would pay her some attention and really become aware of this other existence so close by.

Lenz considered himself an observer of the world, and that was where part of his great strength came from: he had not yet been called to the centre; existence was something he could see—his own just as well as other people's; he was a spectator whose only preoccupation was being fed, getting some sleep, and then the quality of the show. Lenz couldn't hide the fact that he considered himself the only decisive authority in his life. Every other element was secondary to what he considered the key to the problem, the one important problem—which was the fact of being alive. A certain disproportionate adoration that he'd always had for his father was deep down based on an adoration of self-sufficiency, and his parents—the people who had given him the possibility of having the problem of being alive to resolve—were the only people about whom he could never say, *They've never done anything for me*—because the truth was that they had made him, from his head to his toes: a human house.

In relation to his brother, for example, there were no ties of indebtedness at all: they were separate constructions—he and Albert—two parallel houses; one could be without light for years while the other had abundant electricity, coming to despise it like anything we have in excess; so there was nothing between the two houses that might turn *sentimental*.

There had been between the two brothers an irreversible distancing. That is, any approach was an attack and never the prelude to a common handshake.

There was also, meanwhile, the sense of a struggle over a particular space. The material heritage, and also the family name, were the reasons for a repelling the kindnesses that were no more than ways of postponing an explicit conflict. Who had more right to use the family name? That was the most relevant question. Because there was no question here of dividing things up: a name wasn't a piece of land that a reasonably well-meaning measuring tape could split, keeping both sides minimally satisfied. A name cannot be divided up.

And to Lenz the family name was crucial: Buchmann. Lenz Buchmann never showed it off and only didn't insist on being called by his surname because Albert, Albert Buchmann, his brother, older by a few years, had long before him begun to exhibit it himself, as though always setting it down on the table before embarking on any conversation. Lenz would never accept being *the second Buchmann*, not least because he considered that in his brother the name Buchmann had become a defensive name, while in his hands, on the contrary, preceding his own actions, the name Buchmann would take on undeniably warlike features, the features of attack. And this was why he was simply Lenz, likewise addressing his brother by his first name, refusing to make the family surname explicit.

But it was precisely his brother Albert who provoked the change in attitude regarding the letter that the woman about to die had handed Lenz in the hospital.

On a rare visit, always stuffed full of some lecture on literature (both were avid readers), and already having reached the moment when—standing—he was preparing himself for the little insignificant conversations that would precede his departure, Albert saw the letter, still on the stand on the living-room cupboard, with the sender and addressee facing up.

Lenz explained:

"It's a letter from a woman who's dying at the hospital. She gave me the letter to put in the post. She doesn't have long left. I haven't been able to . . ."

Albert frowned, as he always did when faced with any reference to illness, since he himself was ill, and although he seemed still to be in a position of power in relation to the opposing side—that is, death—he saw clearly that it would not be long before the tide of the struggle would turn.

Difficult times," was all Albert said. "Everyone wants to say good-bye."

"Everyone has the right to say good-bye," replied Lenz, dryly.

4

Nature and another kind of prayer

The following day when he looked at the letter, still in the same place, though in a slightly different position now—perhaps a few millimeters farther into the cupboard—he focused on it quite differently. Lenz wasn't thoughtless now, nor was he embroiled in any internal rationalizations or diverted by future concerns. Lenz looked at the letter, saw it clearly, and thought about it.

What could that woman have wanted? Why had she chosen him to take the letter to post?

He was a doctor. Did this woman know that even the most broadly defined duties and chores of a doctor certainly did not include the role of postman? Who did she think she was? The dying demand everything of other people, as though they were new kings, a kind of ill-timed monarchy established not through absolute strength, not by sword or by genealogy, but by the opposite quality: weakness. Acts of compassion couldn't establish monarchies or new kingdoms, thought Lenz, or the city would quickly be swallowed up. Nature is lying in wait out there, still just as strong as it ever was: yes, it has retreated, but it's not even our prisoner. It's just in some other place, at another site in the battle, sharpening its blades; it doesn't pray, it doesn't beg, it doesn't ask for mercy.

It doesn't pray, it sharpens its blades.

5

The kingdom

To Lenz, the letter—that letter, there in front of him—had therefore become unbearable: a symptom of human weakness that was not inconsiderable. It was something that, if allowed to circulate, would come from a great height; the force of gravity would tip it over, and soon the effects of this new element rushing down into the world would become apparent.

That letter was a mild virus, a message that the victors would later keep as a historical example of the foretelling of our fall. Castles began to topple and Kingdoms to lose their strength and the number of their kings was multiplied until they began to be confused with the domestic servants.

The decadence of the human Kingdom was in that letter. Lenz saw this at last.

And it had been his brother, who was himself ill, who no longer went up the mountain with the strategists—he watches them and fears them—it had been his brother who had unintentionally opened Lenz's eyes for him. His brother's compassion for that letter—that alliance of the weak—made it clear what action was required of Lenz. Dr. Lenz, an important surgeon in the city, a man in complete possession of his private pleasures, an appreciator of petty humiliation and prostitutes, and who had lately got into the habit of allowing that tramp into his home, offering him succulent alms, giving him bread and food and, above all, humiliating him, delaying the giving of those alms, the food, savoring the pleasure of being the stronger and having two clear, healthy eyes with which to see what the clarity of the world had to show him: the ugliness of that same world, the violence and the difference between someone with health and someone without, between someone with money and someone without, someone who is old and someone who is not, someone who is ugly or deficient and someone who is not, whose face is marked by an accident, burns, cuts that disfigure their middling beauty and someone on the contrary who had nothing to stain his pride, his external, physical pride, the only currency common to every century, to every country, to every language. It was this that Lenz's clear, healthy eyes could see, it was this that the clarity of the world had to show him.

That letter was not in fact a thing of his world, it was not of his physics, of his science, it did not belong to the world of his amazing special-effects machinery, of those medical techniques that were more and more modern, of high-speed trains, it didn't even belong to the world of animals at its proudest, to the world of strong horses.

The letter was a childish thing, it was from the world that only survives because there's someone or something stronger protecting it. It was from the world of childhood, that was it, and he—Lenz—the surgeon—he had been asked to take on the role of protector. The role of the man who, out of compassion or empathy, takes the letter, sticks on a stamp, and sends it, doing a favor; repeating in a modest way, then, the gesture of a person who takes the hand of someone already beginning to fall from the heights.

However, Lenz didn't like seeing his hand used for such things, actions that are outside the bounds of his competencies, of his profession, his duties as a doctor.

His duty was something quite different. The side where his duty lay, the side wherein he approached, where he pointed his blade, was another side: it was the opposite side from that letter.

Lenz went in another direction; but he lived his life against that letter, and it was against it that he meant to remain alive.

Lenz already knows that all he has to do is make a single gesture and that it was his brother who had played the part of a messenger for him. A stupid messenger, an idiotic messenger, who traveled thousands of kilometers and crossed a dozen dangers to deliver a message he didn't even understand to the other side of the world, a message that actually said the opposite of what he himself would have liked to say. And Lenz received that message, and he—yes— he did understand it.

And so now he does what he knows he has to do. And what he sees not as a casual gesture but as a gesture that fulfills one of his loftiest duties, a gesture that belongs in the deepest part of his Kingdom, the Kingdom to which he swore his loyalty, the King- dom of a man who attacks and who knows that there are elements readying themselves to attack him in return.

Lenz grabs the letter and tears it, once, twice, three times: the letter is destroyed.

DECISIVE MOMENTS

1
The woman dies, but first she asks

Illness in Lenz's brother Albert had quickly become an incredibly arrogant thing: it advanced like a racehorse in second place that feels, so close to the finishing line, that it can still win; an animal, in this case, that does not depend on human will.

In two months the illness had taken on countless new responsibilities within the body—it already controlled various functions, it had invaded and set up military camps in numerous organs; cells were already reorganizing a number of their movements taking into account the orders coming from The Illness and not from the citizen who was falling into it as though falling from the floor to somewhere even lower down. Albert is dying, and his younger brother, Dr. Lenz, has just gone into the room where the hospital keeps bodies during that brief period between the terminal state of dying and the other great state of matter about which we know so little and which is always talked about as though it's a mystery.

Lenz is very familiar with those decisive moments when the possibility of death begins to cancel out every other hypothesis. In fact, Lenz has just come from one of those moments: the woman who had written the letter to her children—a letter which would never reach its destination because days earlier it had itself been transformed into garbage—that woman who had used what remained of her time waiting for a reply or for some other more explicit gesture on the part of her children—a surprise visit, a gift, any sign of effort in order to make contact with a thing with which all contact would soon be impossible—this woman, this sick patient of Dr. Lenz's, had just died in the hospital. And Lenz, as the doctor who had been following the stages of that final decline, and fulfilling his professional duties with absolute rigor, was the person responsible for closing the circle of recorded facts on the existence of the lady in question.

And the final—almost irrelevant—fact in some respects anticipated the monstrous passivity shown by corpses. The woman had asked Dr. Lenz, "Please, close my eyes," and when Lenz closed them, with his right hand, death came, or the lady died.

2
The last Buchmann

Here, then, we find Dr. Lenz facing another decisive moment: his brother Albert is dying.

Lenz could feel two things happening at once: a confusion that revolted him, and—at the same time—a sense of continuity between the previous moment when a body had just died in his hospital (which belonged to the world of his profession—the body of that lady, a woman who was ill, whose suffering he had tried to relieve through every technical means at his disposal), and the present moment when a body being put under pressure by time (time, he felt, was really made up of a mass that could move and exert physical force) was no longer just the former object of his profession but a body with his blood, the body of his brother: that other world of matter which his parents had placed on the earth doubtless in the absurd hope that these descendents would enable them to carry on.

In reality, Albert had never married and had no children, and to Lenz too children were an unnecessary expenditure of energy, an ingenious method for getting someone to lower their rifle. They were projects of love, which ultimately would be hurled into the forefront of all that will be destroyed: no one is worse at hiding than the weak.

Say that his wife, Maria Buchmann, had years ago come to agree with the decision—in Lenz's words—*to staunch the production of weaklings. I don't want some doctor in a future generation to have to save the life of a child with my name.*

A family—and Lenz felt this in his skin—was made up of a large system of hierarchies, protectorates, and compassions that repeated—sometimes more intensely—the linking of varieties of power that exist in an independent Kingdom.

For him, though, the Kingdom would end here.

THE FUNERAL OF ALBERT BUCHMANN

.

1

A mechanism that works

Albert, meanwhile, was already walking paths that were not those of the world of man: four generous military men carried the heavy coffin, on which the symbol of the Party and the symbol of the country were combined—unacceptably, to the eyes of some people—with the flowers that family and friends insisted on leaving.

Lenz and his wife—in subdued formal dress—the color black anticipating the shedding of tears—stood stiffly and formally, in an extraordinary restraint of movement that seems to have been distributed to the rest of those present as well, a secret sign passed from hand to hand delineating which gestures are acceptable, a strange epidemic making some of the most active gentlemen in the city seem ultimately insignificant, rendered worthless by a physical lassitude that puts them in a position of expectation, as though it was of the dead man that great actions were now required.

The corpse of Albert Buchmann, however, was no longer up to performing any great acts, and if there was any activity it was happening somewhere outside the cemetery. From time to time a shout could be heard over the wall, calling out to these active gentlemen who continue respectfully to feign weakness. These were the cries of children who, not yet provided with the faculties that would allow them to understand great events, simply endure, their behavior quite unchanged by whatever turmoil the city might be in.

Lenz received a long series of condolences, as did his wife, who had never been able to bear her brother-in-law, Albert, whom she considered lacking in "great ambitions," though she now eagerly receives every consolation offered by the city's inhabitants. Any of them would have sworn that the woman esteemed her brother-in-law, Albert, highly, such was the emotion with which she received them; at one point the line of people offering condolences had to pause for Lenz to attend to his wife who was weeping copiously.

Let's say that there was nothing at all false about this crying. Lenz's wife was sincere, there was nothing deliberate about it. What it was, though, was a manifestation of the impressive, inherent effectiveness of that mechanism we call a burial. Every person who cried—and several were seen to lower their heads—cried not for the dead man but because of the sound which the wheels of that mechanism gave out. There was—in the religious words being spoken, as much as in the near-universal movements of the soldiers lowering the coffin into the earth—a focus on a point that was common, not individual. The point uniting the community of those present was the feeling that any of them might the following day be the dead man to whom the others would be paying their respects. They were crying collectively for the failure of the city: they had not yet found the antidote to that noise which seemed to be broadcast at every burial. Each man claimed that death—and its *modus operandi*—would end before coming to take him. And at each funeral, saying good-bye to the dead was also a remembering of this common failure, indeed of the failure of humanity's loftiest desire: for its culture, its way of reasoning, to make a new world in which, during peace time, danger would be transformed into an energy that was not normal—extraordinary, even. The truth was, however, that in cities without war, danger may indeed become rare, but as for death, death continues in abundance; it would seem that man is incapable of taking control of its price: this was still low, accessible, like any insignificant product. Death, each individual death, demonstrates cities' economic, technological, and cultural failure.

This was why tears were shed at Albert Buchmann's funeral, just as at any other, not over the individual passing of a body but for the continuous passing of the community of mankind and of their most important project: immortality.

2

What it's possible to spot, out of the corner of your eye

One further change in Lenz's spirits took place during his brother's funeral. And this transformation, so profound, was due to a conjunction of many factors, factors that were imperceptible and which seemed to have no substance to them when analyzed individually, but still came together in his head and in his will, resulting in a crack suddenly opening up in a wall that had previously been intact.

From a certain point onward, what Lenz found most interesting to observe—out of the corner of his eye, during the final phase of the funeral—a phase in which some people had already started leaving—was the way the population approached the president of the city who had kindly shown up at that funeral ceremony.

While he was receiving certain condolences, Lenz observed how people approached that individual who represented power in a totally different way. Many of those who had approached Lenz with condolences, their faces pained, their gestures reserved, speaking words that recapitulated classic, self-contained formulas, Lenz now saw out of the corner of his eye—just minutes later, or even just a few seconds—offering greetings far more energetically (and one might as well admit it: happily), following an exceptionally rapid change, not an external one but a change to the very centre of the organism; those men had taken a leap, like gazelles, in this case a leap in sentimental appearance, but which deep down revealed a social agility that was nothing new: Lenz knew what men were like.

What fascinated him was not the speed with which a citizen moved from sadness to fawning—however controlled, so as to be all the more effective—what fascinated Lenz was the collective way each individual citizen greeted the president of the city in a manner completely different from their approaches to himself. It wasn't the difference between a feigned sadness (for the death of his brother) and then a feigned admiration (for the qualities of the president), it was really a difference between a man presenting himself as an individual or accepting his place as a member of a group. The condolences had been offered by individuals, and those same individuals, a few meters on, had greeted power in the position of soldiers, human elements repeated and cancelling themselves out within a crowd. In that short journey between the brother and sister-in-law of the deceased, and then the president of the city, these men had lost their names, as one might lose a piece of paper out of one's pocket, and when they came to speak, on the other side of this divide, they seemed only capable of echoing the name of the country, of the city, and of its most exalted representatives.

Lenz was never greeted like that, in that manner which he was still wondering about, at some length. Even on other occasions he'd only ever been greeted man to man. Even the mothers whose sons he had saved greeted him as a man—in that case a doctor of remarkable skill; he had never been greeted as though he were a country or a city.

3

A fundamental change in the position of the spirit

In fact, the idea that it was possible to shake hands with a city, since it has a physical component that is multiple, almost infinite, and as such uncontrollable—this was an idea that only sunk in completely during his brother's funeral. What Lenz saw at the exit of the cemetery was a queue of men hiding the mediocrity that the fact of their *being in a line* reveals, through innocuous conversations that really only served to allow time for their moment to arrive. What Lenz saw was a group of men stripped of their individual names, greeting, with their fingers of bone, and yet covered in flesh and blood—these fingers that, while seeming to share the same anatomy, ended nonetheless at the heart of a city—greeting, that is, shaking hands with the city and then moving away, totally sated, as though they had just eaten, just satisfied some organic need. Actually, it was this that most struck Lenz: the men who had just greeted that greatest representative of power moved away in just the same way that he had countless times seen "his" tramp move away after Lenz had given him something to eat. What he saw in those toadying—or just fearful—men was an obvious satisfaction that went from their exteriors, from their faces, down into the deepest cells in their bodies. They moved away, sated with a handshake, replicating the way his tramp moved away after his stomach had disappeared (had been forgotten, that is) after receiving his food and now holding some money in his hands.

What was it, what was it that happened to men? Not just to men's reason but to the organism itself, to their instincts, the things the head can't fully control?

Lenz didn't completely understand the rudiments of this almost magical phenomenon, but at that moment he made a decision—just now, as the area around Albert's plot was emptying out: Lenz was going to join the Party and fight to attain one of its highest positions.

In a sense, the terrain was now clear: his only brother had died. Lenz could finally have exclusive use of the name that publicly proclaimed the strong bloodline from which he had been born. Lenz Buchmann was ready to begin a new life, corresponding to his pride in the rebirth of his surname.

This at a moment when, externally, his autonomous actions were focused upon getting rid of the mud that had stuck to his shoes, scraping one shoe against the other with precise, almost specialized movements; it was there, at that moment, but elsewhere—on the inside—that Lenz decided to abandon medicine completely (there was nothing left to be conquered in that territory) and to enter the world of politics, "the world of great events and great maladies." He was tired of dealing with individuals, and with himself as an individual; that wasn't the right scale for him;

he wanted to operate on the illness of a whole city, not a single, insignificant living being. Above all he wanted to feel *the pleasure of giving that strange food* that power gave to its soldiers and officials, that food that was an almost magical energy, that food which sated the stomachs of the population in a way that wasn't material but just as effective.

A bit of bread and a bit of fear, said Lenz out loud, impulsively, breaking a long period of silence. A phrase that surprised his wife who just a few moments earlier had also plunged into the middle of the now deserted cemetery in an attempt to get the mud off her shoes.

"What did you say, Lenz?" asked his wife, Maria Buchmann.

"Nothing," replied Lenz. "I was thinking about my brother."

A FEW EPISODES IN THE BUCHMANN FAMILY

1

How Lenz grew and became strong

First came his fascination for nature in turmoil, the pleasure of the observer when great storms blow in without warning, quickly overturning the organized system of orderly daytime space.

Besides this, there was the nonexistence, in the head of the family—the father of Lenz and Albert, Frederich Buchmann—of those muscular contractions (many of them invisible) which, when taken together, we call fear.

"In this house, fear is illegal," was one of Frederich Buchmann's more striking sayings.

It was a phrase that, furthermore, was formative for Lenz—his father knew well how important it was to be consistent.

Frederich punished any displays of fear on the part of his sons by locking them in a room in the house—"the prison"—where he would black out the windows, where there wouldn't be a single piece of furniture, not a single object.

On very few (but formative) occasions, Lenz was put in the "prison" for having committed the *illegality* of showing fear. Meanwhile, his brother Albert was always being locked in that space where all play was suspended, and likewise all attack or defense. It was an utterly neutral space, where the function of gestures was cancelled out—movement was unnecessary, almost ridiculous. The walls weren't stimulating surfaces for a human being—still less if this human being was a child. It was thus a space that crushed childhood—a heavy weight crushing an object far less robust; it was impossible in that space to act or even to think in accordance with one's age.

The periods spent in "prison" were short. Sometimes not even twenty minutes would go by, and only in the worst cases would it stretch to a few hours. But if Frederich Buchman's pedagogical activity had one major characteristic, it was symbolized by this "gestureless space" (as Frederich called it).

To the Buchmann family, the great disturbance in the development of personality really came from fear. Frederich Buchmann used to say:

"I can hear any accusation about you, you can commit the most immoral acts, you can have the police coming after you, or even the devil himself; I will defend my sons with any weapon I have. I will only be ashamed if I hear that you have been afraid. If that happens, don't bother to come running here: you will find this door closed to you."

This was the environment in which Lenz lived. He learned to exist like this. He prepared himself, he grew, he became strong.

2

There is no order in nature

The two brothers were opposites in personality: both uncommonly intelligent, and cultured to an above-average standard thanks to their father's rich library, which fed their taste for reading, but really Lenz and Albert were from quite different worlds. Lenz did not just fight, he sought out combat—like his father, as it happened—while Albert, who had inherited some traces of their mother, recoiled, skirted round any enemy. And he would skirt around his enemy whether it was a dangerous physical object—a wall too high to jump—or a schoolmate who had provoked him. Lenz sometimes found himself fighting in his big brother's name, with a mixture of brotherly feeling and—mainly this latter—a physical and instinctive attraction to fighting itself.

Besides this, the attraction toward moments when nature changes had also passed quickly from the father down to his younger son, Lenz. Frederich tried, over the course of the boys' education, to show how nature, on regular days, was a slow machine, that seemed like any other that man had invented; nature seeming also to depend on levers shaped like the human hand.

Frederich pointed into the garden, at his gardener, who had long ago begun his physical decline, and told his sons that this was the perfect example of what nature is in peace-time: even an illiterate old man, with little strength in his arms, unable to say a single sensible thing, even a man like that, *a secondary man*, was able to control a garden, that other machine, that green machine.

But from early on, Frederich also drew his sons' attention to the other side of nature, the moment when nature becomes a warrior—"It's only then that it's worth taking photographs," he used to say. In those moments—during a storm, for example—when rapid changes replace slow changes, what rises to the surface is the moral incompatibility—if we can use that word, "moral"—between the system of men and the system of nature. Ultimately what was a crime in one is no crime in the other.

Which was why, argued Frederich, the nature we cohabit with on regular days, on its "weak days," is a deception.

And this is the deception: on a peaceful, sunny day, you open your window and look out at what was not made specifically for man's intelligence, and you look at it with all the benevolence you bring to bear upon a series of paintings arranged on a museum wall. That is precisely where the mistake lies, in looking at nature as though it were a living museum, a museum whose exhibits shift position almost imperceptibly, as though they were the product of these objects' shyness, or simply their weakness. On the days when what is not human can be cut up into pieces, just like a machine can be broken up into its component parts, on such days, when a man can feel proud to clean his shoes on a world that existed before him, yes, then nature really *is* a museum.

Sometimes, however, the objects in the museum show themselves to be parts of a secret artillery, show that they had just been waiting for the right moment to reorganize themselves according to their other aims. And so all of a sudden something that seemed to have been created for one purpose—contemplation (people needed cinema, of course, and nature seemed to be the film chosen by God to screen uninterruptedly before their eyes)—that which can be viewed with a relaxed attitude, even to the point of arranging a few chairs to take in the sunrise, or the sunset, or the falling snow—this thing that seemed to be no more than a weak ally is transformed in seconds into the strongest of enemies.

And this because its weapons are not understood: a storm that hurls trees and people to the ground, swallows up houses and pets; a sea that—lit by energies that seem to belong to some domain beyond reason—drowns boats and men, accompanied by the grotesque sounds of those lightning-flashes, sounds that reveal a fundamental ailment, a failure to conform with the calm and safety of the city, where buildings as instruments for defending against cataclysms become ridiculous when the true forces of this false museum are unleashed; the feeling, in short, that man, at such times, wrapped up in the absurd, would even pick up a hammer to fight a fire, not as a lunatic might, but as though deprived, quite simply, of his technical reason, not even remotely understanding the mechanism of the forces now attacking. To summarize: nothing is understood by the men defending themselves. Hence the clear position of fragility in the face of unhinged nature.

3

Why is it that things that are so close to us can't speak?

In the little monarchical State that was the Buchmann family, Lenz was by far the best prepared to receive the crown when the time came for it to be passed on. Albert, in fact, didn't even want it.

It was Albert, however, who was the older Buchmann, and age revealed traces of other not-easily-explained forces that counterbalanced the actions of each one's existence.

Frederich looked at Lenz with pride, and at Albert sometimes with shame and even revulsion. From his mother Albert had inherited a caution combined with a spirit of unconfrontational sacrifice—that is, he was made to suffer (though no one there was afraid of suffering), but he bore this suffering in defensive positions, and never clear and offensive ones.

The fact of Albert having been born earlier than his brother meant that Frederich did not take any clear decision regarding the passing on of his estate: the order of one's birth was the language of a universal force that—precisely because it couldn't quite be defined or understood in all its particulars—demanded significant respect. If Albert had come first, there was a reason for it—so said the head of the Buchmann family to himself occasionally, trying to argue in defense of the more cautious of his sons.

But he had no doubts about their behavior:

"I have a dog and a wolf," Frederich Buchmann used to say, directly, to his sons.

And though he didn't say it, just thinking it, more and more often, whenever he felt unable to keep such vigorous guard over his family for too much longer, he worried that their two opposing personality types would make any alliance impossible: the dog couldn't protect the wolf because he didn't have the strength, and the wolf would never protect the dog because such behavior is not in his nature.

INTO THE PARTY

1

Initial reactions. Big world, small world.

Lenz's entry into the Party was received with surprise, surprise replaced immediately by enthusiasm on the parts of the city's prominent personalities. Lenz was one of their foremost doctors, and their surprise could be attributed precisely to that same fact: how was it that someone who had reached the highest level of competence in their particular function could abandon it without any warning? Because the statement he made to the press was perfectly explicit: "Lenz Buchmann hereby announces that he is definitively giving up his career as surgeon in order to dedicate himself to the problems of the city," and this announcement fed countless conversations held on the sidewalks along the main roads of the city, where Lenz now made a point of loitering so as to be seen, signaling a return to the streets, essentially giving the impression of someone who had been trapped for years and years in operating theaters, in rigorously hygienic sealed compartments, and who now felt the absolute necessity for some fresh, pure air. Despite the fact that what hospital buildings actually try to do is filter out the *bad air* from the streets through artificial processes.

So what Lenz breathed, then, with a certain amount of delight, was the smoke from all the machines, infiltrating the sky, and in this conflict between smoke and sky—or else this ambiguous truce between those two elements—Lenz also saw blue smoke in the sky, a deliberately provoked color rather than a spontaneous color, since it was denying its opponent—that is, nature— the possibility of a force and of a will.

At the same time, Lenz was pleased with the new vocabulary that he was conquering bit by bit at Party meetings and in the conversations he'd been having with "robust" citizens; citizens who greeted him, who praised his qualities as a doctor, and were amazed at his decision to surrender to the city: "I'm sure you'll earn half of what you were earning," or "You won't make any money," were repeated in a whisper, and even repeated to his face—by those who wanted to subjugate him right away. Some citizens—in disbelief—went so far as to doubt his decision: "It won't be long before he's back doing surgery," or "The family money will last a good few generations yet," etc. etc.

To those who predicted a return to his former life—because the Party had never really wanted to allow in new people or new thoughts—or to those who predicted he would soon be worn down by the vast scale of his new work and so return to the small spaces of the hospital, to these people, Lenz would reply, amused:

"I've promised myself I won't be back in the hospital until I'm there as a patient."

And at this, everyone around him would laugh.

A NEW POSITION IN THE WORLD

1

The number of people who recognize you when you cross the street

Lenz's life changed. Not entirely, of course, but in just a few months it became clear that he was entering a new system, a new science that was not medical science, in which the confrontations are physical ones and in a certain sense only involve two subjects—doctor and patient—and as such are individual, exclusive confrontations. Only two months after giving up medicine, Lenz Buchmann was already seeing a kind of egotism in that sort of activity, and at the same time an excess of humility, as everything that a doctor did he did without any spectators, or at most with very few—specialized technicians as spectators, his professional colleagues or auxiliary staff, or else spectators who were, so to speak, affectively specialized: the close relatives of the patients who were sometimes present for the less significant medical procedures. Such specialist spectators actually made up—and he could now see this quite clearly—only a tiny number, a minority. Two months after embarking on some political activity within the Party there were already more people who knew about him than in fifteen years of his work as a doctor. And what is most important is that Lenz Buchmann had no doubt whatsoever that he had been an exceptionally competent and effective doctor, while in his new political activities he felt he was still in his apprenticeship. In short, a novice, in spite of—over these few weeks—having noticed that his organism had long ago demanded that he take up such activities, which was why with each day that passed he felt himself on the verge of taking on some of the current made up of the citizens of the city, on the verge of taking hold of something in the same way one might pick up an object, an object that subsequently, in one's hands, turns into a sort of key. That's what he felt just about to take hold of.

It was in that apparent chaos of human traffic and possible decisions that Lenz discovered the existence of a central point in what he called the energy of control. There was, deep down, a question of technique, just as had faced him in his former life when standing at the operating table. So, just as in a delicate operation, certain preliminary gestures were indispensable to making the decisive gesture effective—*there is always a final touch that saves or fails to save*, Lenz used to say—and likewise in the collective operation that was politics, in this act (which is almost monstrous when you consider its dimensions) that put thousands of people under the scalpel of a single political decision, in this gigantic *medical operation* there was also an elementary technique that—while not directly implying the salvation or death of an individual organism—did touch some sensitive spots: the seats of men's fear and admiration. Locations that, for many people—as Lenz had learned early from his father—were often confused.

The great advantage of Lenz's switching systems was undoubtedly the number of people he was now able to influence—or even to touch, in the physical sense, in the sense of a scalpel interfering with tissue. Lenz felt like a soldier who had put down his pistol—a pistol that retains a kind of circumscribed effectiveness, the single effect of an individual hatred—in order then to sit down at the controls of a bomber, which in a single second can transform an entire city, and with it ten or twenty centuries, into ruins.

This surprising possibility of reducing a large space and a long stretch of time to an empty, black dot, the possibility of eliminating centuries—churches, for example, containing relics that they claimed came from Christ himself—this ability to *eliminate time* had always fascinated Lenz (an explosion destroys space, and so time as well, clearly), partly having caught this fascination from his father Frederich, who—having been a soldier—late in life lamented only having been able to give orders to bring down each enemy organism one by one, not having been born later, at a time when a single word of command could eliminate and burn off significant portions of the map. In the past we had weapons that interfered with organs or—at most—with families, now we have weapons that interfere with countries, so said the retired soldier Frederich, bemoaning this failure of synchrony between his own personal physical strength, which was now declining in his old age, and the weapons that each day were gaining in reach and power.

2

Medicine and war: two ways of using your right hand

Lenz no longer found it odd that all his thoughts ended up in military images. The fundamental structure of his education had been supplied by a military man—his father—and Lenz still retained an admiration for the urgent sort of excitement that combat instilled in every man, and which his father, Frederich, had passed on to him. There is no woman in the world—Frederich Buchmann used to say—who can excite you as much as the possibility that you will kill a man whom (for whatever reason) you hate at that particular moment.

In any case, Lenz Buchmann had wandered into medicine by chance, a decision resulting from a temporary bout of optimism and not from the desolation he felt in relation to the rest of humanity, and which was at the root of his thoughts and of his very existence. He was someone who had been born and educated to kill and through intellectual aimlessness had decided to practice medicine. Paradoxically he chose to save men one by one, since it would be obscene—or merely inadequate—to kill many at a time when this imperative was suspended, since the time for him to choose a profession had coincided with the ending of the war; or to be more precise, with an intermission, since, a few years later, it—that is, the war—would return.

Meanwhile, deep down, even in those many years when he practiced medicine, Lenz had been a military man. Someone with a taut sense of his duties, and who always thought out all the ramifications of a given decision—and he was well aware that any resolution, once applied, should be followed through to its end, without any indecision or weakness. He knew that he couldn't at the last moment simply change the direction of the scalpel, or of a bullet, since that's how mistakes happen, major errors—those sins that are not only technical in nature, but moral too: striking, for example, due to some failing, an ally rather than an enemy.

Frederich Buchmann's ethics on this matter were also clear, and Lenz had absorbed them completely: *Anyone who accidentally kills a friend, if he is an honorable man, will then take his own life. But killing a friend through a conscious decision, that means you've already chosen the path of the devil, and once that happens, there is nothing for it but to keep on going.*

"Don't be fooled by the speed of the traffic," Frederich Buchmann said once to his two sons, Lenz and Albert, something he repeated subsequently many times to his wolf son alone, Lenz. The most important thing, Frederich Buchmann would say, is not the speed of the machine in which we're sitting, but of the decisions we make. A speed that depends entirely on the organism, on the blood you receive when you're born and the ideas you receive as you grow. That's the real speed, Frederich used to say, the speed at which you decide. Compared to that, a plane is about as fast as an old cart.

3

A suicide that Lenz will not forget

Now that his brother had died, Lenz couldn't stop thinking about how strange it was that the two of them had grown up hearing the same things being said and taking in the same ideas and yet turned out so different. And Lenz saw in the origin of this division between *two systems* the determining influence of blood, which was why he was constantly blaming his mother, in his mind, for his brother's weakness. It was from her that Albert had inherited a way of living that couldn't be measured by the same gauge as his father's life, or Lenz's own.

And now that Albert's existence had come to an end, Lenz could say that it hadn't just been his way of living—his excessive politeness, his hygienic delicacy, never wanting to be any bother—this wasn't the only thing that his brother had inherited from the female side of the family: his illness, too, which had weakened him slowly at first and then at a rate reminiscent of the speed of recent technology, a rapid transfer of information between death and what little life remained in Albert's organism; this death, then, this way of dying that was so like his way of living, was also—without a doubt—feminine. His illness had come from his mother's side and furthermore had been accepted without a struggle, or at least not one that Lenz could see.

Lenz the doctor had often told people that someone who is ill mustn't merely defend himself from his illness but also attack it, just as he—the doctor—attacked it, with a weapon in his fist: to cut off its head. And it was this soldierly instinct, always wanting to gain ground and not just keep the ground already conquered, that he had never seen at the end of Albert's life, after the effects of the illness had finally become visible.

Albert sought shelter in the territory he already knew, when he should have been seeking shelter right in the city of the enemy, right in the enemy camp, if possible just a few hundred meters from the opposing general, who was then devising the best strategy for annihilating Albert's side; we should indeed seek out a hiding place, but only the better to aim at that general's head.

His brother's lack of mental and physical discipline, the way he reduced his actions to a minimum, seeming to regress into more and more embryonic states—like someone who hadn't even been born yet—the way he accepted the progress of his illness, seeming to respect (with no objections) its new system of laws, imposed from the outside in, as though he wasn't the master of his own life; Lenz had found all this shocking.

Illness—Lenz had always thought—was not a courageous way to die, and his activities as a doctor, sometimes even saving men who were right on the edge, were ultimately a way of giving even these organisms a little dignity. *It's not right for a strong man to allow himself to die because of the actions of a few cells*, Frederich used to tell his son Lenz, and Lenz, years later, used to tell his patients. *Lead*—Frederich would say to his two sons—*lead is what kills a Buchmann.*

His father, as ever, carried out this order, which in a sense he had imposed upon himself, and which was ultimately to be so important—at a certain moment, which will come later—in the life of his son, Lenz.

Two days before turning fifty-eight, beginning his physical decline, Frederich Buchmann killed himself with a bullet to the head.

It was an episode that no son—however strong he may be—could ever forget.

POSITIONS IN THE WORLD (INVENTORY)

1

Order and money in the pocket

To Lenz, Albert had left his life "childlike," or "virgin-like." And this basic lack of elegance, this devaluation, so to speak, of the family's most important currency—honor and courage—meant that Lenz felt absolutely no qualms about speedily acquiring all his brother's belongings. The old house of Albert Buchmann—the brother whom Lenz, from the moment of Albert's death, tried to get everyone to refer to by his first name alone, effacing all connection to their surname, as though simply forgetting to mention it—this house had been sold in less than six months, while some parcels of Albert's land that had appreciated in value were held onto, pending "the right weather for selling," to quote Lenz, who associated rises and falls in currency, economic crises and euphorias, with a series of factors that operated more or less at random, not under man's control, mysterious mechanisms that consequently resembled variations in climate and their own unpredictability.

In this regard, the city, in order to distribute wealth and make the most of it, seemed to depend on some sort of external will.

There was, deep down, a sense that even after so much progress, after so many extraordinary technological innovations, man still depended on whether or not a tree bore fruit, even if there were no longer any trees or fruits being picked or gathered from the ground, but simply negotiated over. So where was a new tree to be found? And what was it, this tree that made prices rise so suddenly and hunger descend onto various parts of the country, only to begin, later, after a few years had gone by, and with no good reason, to bear fruit in excess?

In a way, Lenz's entry into the Party and his coming closer, therefore, to the spaces and times so decisive for his country were also connected to the feelings—simultaneously erotic and military—aroused by his curiosity. He wanted to see whether being closer to whoever was making decisions affecting the entire population would allow himself to understand—like someone finally finding the last piece in a puzzle—the logic of the fluctuations of wealth. Perhaps what in his former professional life (the life of an individual facing individuals, *the life of one to one*, as he called it) he had interpreted as anarchic, disordered, and lacking a coordinating general—society's economic and military fluctuations—did in fact have an unambiguous leader, a clear starting point, a mechanical rhythm and velocity: adaptable, repeatable. In this *one-to-many* position—the new battleground on which Lenz was accomplishing his forceful entry into the Party—perhaps he might be able to find a logic, causes: the fundamentals in what had previously seemed to be utter chaos.

This was a secondary interest compared to his obsession with the energy that came from power, which had so fascinated him at his brother's funeral, but it was still in his sights: understanding to what extent the composition of the substances that make up political power affect the trajectories and speed of the circulation of money. Lenz wanted confirmation of what his father had taught him: *the general's word of command determines how much money the soldier's son will one day have in his pocket.*

Lenz the adolescent, and later Lenz the doctor, had grown fascinated by this sentence; and now it was time for a distinguished politician—Lenz Buchmann—to understand what was at its roots. Though this particular investigation was, necessarily, secondary; if his father said it, he trusted it to be so.

It should be mentioned that Lenz always interpreted his father's simple ideas about the world as absolutely direct statements, or even imperatives. And it was always easier for Lenz to force the world to occupy precisely the position his father had appointed it than ever admit that his father might have been wrong. Lenz knew how to take an order. Its consequences might be good or bad, but that all comes later and is besides the point, is unrelated to the energy contained in the order itself. An order is—simply—a phrase that must be obeyed, a piece of language; and whoever receives it should make it a reality—and pay the price with his life, if necessary. An order expresses the will of a person who knows more than you, and consequently there should be a series of movements corresponding to that word of command, movements that seek to align the world with the clear-sighted vision of the person who gave it. Each time an order is fulfilled completely, it is a confirmation of the pre-existing hierarchy, and thus the heart is calmed.

2

Being never so close

Given his intellectual capabilities—the flexibility of his culture compared to those of the men who were now his peers, monopolized and dominated by certain fixed ideas—Lenz Buchmann rose quickly in the Party. Lenz Buchmann—spoken just like that, always: the surname had become a requirement; the syllable "Lenz" had developed an appetite—it was like someone out in the audience wanting another person in the seat next to him, so as to have some company while watching the world. "Lenz" was merely a lookout post, which gained new significance by association with his surname.

So Lenz quickly learned a new discipline. Not a new kind of mathematics or a new kind of physics, but the old science of joining men and separating them. It's true that these petty alliances and tiny declarations of war were far removed from the ideal forms such activities might take, but, nonetheless, Lenz saw how all human relationships within the Party operated according to these same principles. Used to dealing single-handedly with bodies whose cells have turned vengefully against them, Lenz now "had more people alongside him." His medical team in the more complicated operations he performed never exceeded seven people, but now he found himself at meetings where his every statement would be taken in by dozens of colleagues from the Party. Political meetings gave off a sort of magnetic energy, uniting (or separating) every member of a group, linking its constituent parts, from one end to the other.

This sense of community was a new invention of Lenz's era, the era when Lenz was making his entrance into politics. The Party members supposedly didn't share an ethos—that is, these were men supposedly coming from entirely different bloodlines, from families who had never shared a bed, had never benefited or suffered from the same declarations of surrender or victory, but were now standing side by side, as though they had been fighting in the same army for centuries.

Lenz was in no way blinded by this illusion—for illusion is what it was. Even during those meetings when the terrain seemed to acquire a unique physiognomy, and when the need for connection between the attendees approached the limit beyond which nothing but physical love could sate them, Lenz kept himself ambivalent: there he was, in the thick of things, sharpening his weapons with the others, but at the same time he was up there at the lookout post, a secret, hidden place, and—why not say it?—a place for betrayal: from there he could see not into the enemy camp but into the camp of his own allies.

It's hardly irrelevant that Lenz had listened to countless stories told by his father in which two soldiers, or a soldier and an officer, take advantage of circumstances that leave them alone together—

completely isolated from the rest of their army, one shooting the other in the back to enact some personal revenge, later claiming that there had been an ambush in which the other had regrettably fallen. In these stories, which his father told, Lenz intuited something of significance: the victor, in these cases, was always alone, always one—not two, not three, not twenty—one—and nothing, not ever, would change this.

When you kill someone from your own army, for reasons that are purely individual, it becomes apparent that you nurture far less hatred for an enemy of your country or his ideas than you'll ever develop for a personal enemy. Personal hatred has a potency that cannot be matched.

3

A confession that would have countless consequences

It was around that time that Frederich Buchmann recounted a significant episode from his life, one of the rare occasions when he described a concrete detail of his participation in the war. He had only told his son Lenz—and then only when Lenz was already grown up. They were walking together through the city. It wasn't a confession, it was a neutral account, in which he himself—Frederich—seemed no more than a witness to a road accident for which he had no responsibility and in which he had no emotional involvement. His father told him he had killed a soldier from his own army.

"With my own hand I reduced my regiment's assets," as he put it himself.

And why? Just this: "His look," said father Frederich. And he went on:

"It was because of this—when there was a moment when the two of us were alone—that I killed him. In the report I said that, through carelessness, he had managed to kill himself with his own weapon. And it was true: the bullet did come from his own gun. Only I was the one who fired it.

"His look, whenever he received an order from me," Lenz's father insisted, "that was why. You might say that's nothing too critical—now, many years later, surrounded by all the trappings of peace. But in wartime orders are critical, they're fundamental, and there are looks people give you that can have consequences. If he'd had the chance, he would have done the same to me. After that look, I just acted faster than him. Either he didn't notice my look in return or he was just slower. Or perhaps—this is the third possibility—he just didn't want to reduce the regiment's assets . . ." and here, Frederich Buchmann laughed.

On several occasions Lenz would recall this story, both as a way of dampening his enthusiasm, the intoxication that feelings of fraternity caused him—it seemed sometimes that the connection between two men could be eternal—and then for another reason, another detail, about which we will speak in due course.

In fact, Lenz never forgot the name of the soldier his father had killed. Actually, it had been his own curiosity that had disinterred the name:

"What was he called, Father?"

"Who?"

"The soldier."

"There are certain names you don't particularly want to keep in your head," replied Frederich.

"Tell me what he was called."

"I don't remember his first name; his surname was Liegnitz."

The name resounded like a little explosion in Lenz's head, and he immediately recalled it when the president—two days after Lenz Buchmann had been elected by his comrades in the Party to an important city post—introduced him to a young woman, a twenty-five year old, who from that point on was to be his secretary:

"My dear Dr. Lenz Buchmann, let me introduce you to your new secretary; extraordinarily competent, I can assure you: Julia Liegnitz."

THE LIBRARY

1

How can you tame an animal without a firm hand?

The retrieval by Lenz—following his brother's death—of the half of their father's library that had ended up in Albert's house, brought Lenz's body a feeling of rescue, completely overwhelming the sense that he was a thief, or even the feeling that he'd somehow struck a beneficial deal at just the moment when the other negotiator was too weak to protect his interests. The character of Frederich Buchmann's library was in its totality; more than that, as a whole it made up one of the most significant elements of his father's character. So to Lenz, the sharing of the library with his brother after their father's death had been an act of absolute violence.

It was this incident, in fact, that had definitively distanced Lenz and Albert. They were both great readers, and so both were quite interested in that exceptional trove, with its thousands of books. To Lenz, however, that library was more than just the sum total of its contents: hovering there in that library was the figure of the patriarch of the Buchmann family. There was a sort of lone ghost, quite incompatible with any statistical frame of mind, that linked all those volumes, and which transformed the common sharing-out of "one for you, one for me" into a technical exercise which by a certain point had taken so long that it started to become obscene.

That day Lenz had felt a perfectly clear hatred for his brother, who had forced him to set aside his fighting spirit—retreating from battle, settling for half—with a grocer's logic, measuring each square meter (like the unit of any collection, whether a book or a work of art) and bringing the entire affair into the world of the balancing scales, of fair and moral distribution, which resembles justice—which is, after all, not a human concept but a numerical one.

As if justice could not find expression in excess, as if a scale balanced evenly on each side wasn't just a form of stinginess, humiliating each party by treating them as equivalents.

On that grave day, Lenz did even try saying, "A library like this shouldn't be split up," hoping that his brother might consider adopting the posture of someone lowering his weapon in submission in order to allow his opponent to keep his raised. And yet Albert (as Lenz realized that day) wasn't only weak, soft by nature, but also unable to make a true sacrifice. At that moment—thought Lenz later—Albert must have had the sense that what was at stake was not who would keep a certain work by a certain writer but who would keep their father's unfinished work. It was a matter of finding out who would grip the hammer—still raised—and then quickly and powerfully bring to an end the well-aimed blow that their father, Frederich Buchmann, had begun.

It was really a matter of their father's legacy, but the library was not a material inheritance in the classic sense: it was a position, a form of morality.

Albert must have known, however, that the movement, the continuation required by the library wasn't something that he could provide. His father's library had begun a series that would have its own natural continuity. There was a gap in intensity between each of the books, and it was necessary to get to know that gap, to get to the core of it in order to be able to continue with the library, taking it in hand and leading it along the same path, like a horse to be broken—brutally, if need be, but with a precise objective in sight. The library wasn't a passive object, it wasn't a thing wanting to be put into order. Quite the contrary, it was a living thing that needed taming, leading; a horse, yes, that was the perfect image, a horse that even after years of working for the family still retains—deep down within its organism—an instinct which is not human (and which is also quite human), the instinct to dislike man; feeling its muzzle and shoes to be incompatible with the work a common man demands at the end of a tiring day.

Their father's library had not concluded its demands. In that sense, the invitation to act—which walking through its shelves instilled in Lenz—was absolutely clear.

But what was to be made of these invitations to do battle with his brother, Albert, for whom reading was a leisure activity, and not one of those rare moments when the world's strategy of attack starts to become clear? For Albert, old age would be when he would at last be able to read more often; whereas Lenz, on the other hand, would abandon reading in old age, because reading demands a vitality that only someone capable of acting forcefully on the world is able to provide.

What would my father think of me, Lenz would often murmur, after his father's death, in just those moments when a curtain seemed to open over the day and the sun emerged, as though it were simultaneously a word of command capable of uniting all things beneath it and the source of all discord. What would he think of me?

2

How do you separate two energies that are no longer visible?

Lenz did the whole job alone. Albert's funeral had been the previous day.

A gap of no more than a day. There was Lenz, going into his brother's library, trying to separate the original books from his father's library from the books that Albert had subsequently—or previously—acquired himself.

He separated those books, and he saw them as different, opposite, like sickness and health, like a weapon and a shield, a man waking up and a man falling asleep. Lenz had a feeling of attraction or repulsion that drew him toward or pushed him away from each volume, depending on its owner. There was no sign here of a separation between good books and books by authors who were mediocre or transient. Nothing of the sort. Brother Albert had also been a solidly cultured man, a man who knew which books weighed down a shelf and which seemed to float, seeming barely there at all, just air, an element to which one pays no attention. There were no books of that kind, insubstantial books, in Albert's house. But what mattered was the impulse of the person who had bought them. The act of leaving his brother's books and taking only those that had belonged to his father's library determined a hierarchy, which was not literary but existential. It wasn't a matter of the lines that an eye could read in a given book, but the way one's hands held it.

Lenz did in fact recall a harsh reprimand from his father, on a day when, after a pause, Frederich had said roughly to him—as though Lenz were about to break some symbolic family jewel or to fall from a high precipice—

"Don't hold a book like that."

3

Recovering original potential: not everyone holds things in the same way

He was no longer a child when this had happened, he had graduated, there were already many people who addressed him with unsophisticated delicacy as *Doctor Lenz*. So Doctor Lenz looked with some surprise at his father, then heard him say:

"You don't cling to a book like that the same way you cling to the hand of your fiancée, understand?"

Lenz understood. And later, after many years had passed, here he was proving it. The books—and not only that one book—were marked by the hands that had originally held on to them, and it was this mark that he was looking for. In his brother's library there were books marked by those warlike hands, and there were books that just weren't. And it was easy to tell the difference—like the wheat from the chaff, thought Lenz, with a smile of unmistakable cruelty, a smile that was unusual in someone like him who knew better and better how to temper the inscriptions that the inside of his body might make on the outside, on reality. But he was alone, in the middle of the library, in an almost melancholy late afternoon. He could smile like that, he had no one observing him, except for God, and he was doubtful of His competence as an eyewitness. There was something that just didn't work about this God. A sort of incomplete totality, like someone who's already put on an impeccable suit to wear to his wedding and then when he comes at last to put on his shoes finds himself—without noticing, without emotion—wearing two perfect shoes, but two shoes for the same foot, two right shoes. The truth was, as Lenz said himself, he wasn't going to allow himself to be intimidated by blind people.

But at that moment he was disgusted—that was the word—with the way Albert had dared to mix his own books in with their father's.

Albert hadn't kept his father's library isolated on some particular shelves, with his own on others; on the contrary, he had merged all authors, reordered everything, arranged it all alphabetically, a simplistic decision that revealed the flaws in his character—he confused strength with alphabets.

And there they were, two antagonistic worlds artificially united into a single world, a kind of crazy paradise in which wolves and dogs come together to graze the same pastures as well-behaved sheep. Dear old Albert, thought Lenz, your death wasn't enough: I'm also going to find it easy to forget you.

Albert's books were marked by an irreversible decadence, as of a train that, having left the tracks, falls uncontrollably through the mysterious space, now untamed, which had previously surrounded the technical marvel of its engine so patiently. Lenz's brother Albert was someone whom nature had rejected—the same way a bad student is rejected by a man-made institution: his brother's books had the mark, and the smell, of his illness. They were civilized volumes, but fragile ones. They were something that had been sterilized, the room of a sick man.

As for Lenz: he was from another world entirely.

4

Forgettings and derisory debts

The library that Lenz had rescued and was now arranging inside, "in the belly," of his own library—already made up of his own books and then some of his father's, all mixed together, since there was no difference between the current down which each one flowed: his body carried his father's mark, his hands seemed to bear the same furrows made by the weapon used by brave officer Frederich Buchmann during the war—his father's library, then, seemed now to have been reconstituted, to be recovering its strength by way of some mysterious process.

What Lenz felt was that he was the *only* real son of Frederich Buchmann: what was being fulfilled now was a requirement demanded by the books themselves. True brothers were being brought back together, and this process of reunion gave off a powerful energy. Rare books by the same author, first editions, were now side by side; they had lived apart for a few years, separated—like a divorce—and now they were celebrating their reunion, the fusion of two spaces into one. The books demonstrated a companionship that was absolutely incomparable: as they came back together they seemed to be putting on a new uniform, each of them, as though they had been demobilized and were now—just by simple touch, skin against skin—being mobilized once more, soldiers grouping together to reconquer the paternal home.

This companionship between books surprised and thrilled Lenz Buchmann, now that it's clear that he is the only Buchmann (in the world of the living, that is, and of humans, and even the speechless world of nature), the only one who carries within himself the characteristics of those who judge other people and not the characteristics of those who are judged.

His father's library is at last in its place: in the house of his son, Lenz, the son who would in future be the oldest child, despite not having been born in that order, as in a few years he would be overtaking the age Albert was when he died.

And this is no simple anxiety—of overtaking in life the age of someone who has died; it's a necessity, a way of breaking with the past, a way of forgetting that becomes not a neglect but an active chore. Lenz Buchmann needed to forget that he had a brother, Albert, who had lived and died weak, who lived and died not like a Buchmann but like an observer of the Buchmann family.

Someone content to remain mediocre; he lived wanting health, then died running through every degree of illness, a good and obedient man who never protested climbing up to the gallows so as not to interrupt the show.

And then, at last, what came was death, which was not—as it is not for any coward—the same terror that it is to strong men.

Lenz will forget his brother, in just the way he forgets to pay a derisory debt. So the debt simply remains, because no one is so indelicate as to trouble another person to recover something so trivial.

5

A little weakness on the part of Lenz Buchmann

Lenz has just arranged the final volume. He is standing looking at every part of the room.

The library is once again united and in motion. And it is he, now, who is the possessor of the word of command, of the voice that says, "I want that one! And that one! And that one!"

An ancient electrical current runs through it—not a weak current, just an ancient one. Which only means that it started earlier. And this current now has someone who knows how to grab hold of it, to get it moving again. This invisible thing is utterly violent, thinks Lenz, this thing running between the books, between every pair of books, an energy that has no name save the name of its owners, Lenz Buchmann and the brave officer Frederich Buchmann.

And for once Lenz feels like he's being attacked with no time to respond. He leans on one of the shelves, lowers his head, and for the first time since his father's death does what he hadn't even done at the funeral of that man who had put a bullet in his head the moment he realized that weakness—unmannered and indelicate— was taking charge of him. Surrounded by a library that had been reconstituted and that is happy at last, and that is only incomplete because it wants more and not because it's lacking anything, in the late afternoon, a day after the insignificant funeral of his brother Albert, Lenz thinks of his father and cries; forgetting for that moment that he is strong Lenz, the only son whose hand bears the mark of the weapon of the officer Frederich Buchmann.

ON MEN

1

Julia and Gustav Liegnitz

Julia Liegnitz, secretary to the fastest-rising politician in the Party, Lenz Buchmann, was indeed competent.

The connection between the two of them accelerated due to a series of urgent activities that the Party placed in the hands of this new public figure.

With her devotion to the aim of efficiently carrying out his decisions, the connection between this man, already powerful, enormously cultured, and married too, and this young woman who was clearly just starting out in every way, still apparently naïve about various matters, among them her own capacity for suffering and other people's, this connection, then, was strengthened almost mechanically—here was a structure made of steel with a shape that was unshakeable and in which another small piece, though one which could still be molded, would now be inserted.

Just like any other secretary, Julia Liegnitz wrote letters, was the first contact for second-rank petitioners so that Dr. Buchmann shouldn't waste any time *listening to the personal convictions* of uninteresting people, she answered the telephone, selected relevant pieces of information from the newspapers, and, above all, maintained that discrete modesty Lenz felt that any good personal servants ought to uphold.

She kept a distance that was there not to allow the possibility of a sudden leap, but instead to encourage one's coming closer step by tiny step, giving the impression of not wanting to awake some terrible, slumbering thing. This was the position held by Julia—and, frankly, Lenz liked it.

To her this tendency toward attentiveness—at its most extreme almost subservience—came quite naturally.

As to the surname that had so startled Lenz on the day they were introduced, there was no longer any doubt; he had had no trouble investigating: she was the daughter of the soldier who had died in combat, in the regiment commanded by officer Frederich Buchmann. This soldier, who Lenz now knew was called Gustav Liegnitz, had left two orphan children: Julia, the eldest, and a boy who was now twenty years old and whom the soldier Gustav Liegnitz had never even seen. This kid, who had been born after the news arrived of his father's death in combat, had been given the name that was to be expected in such a situation, exactly the same name as his father: Gustav Liegnitz.

2

Rescuing beggars

Lenz's change of scale had been so quick that, at first, he found it difficult to recognize certain men he had dealt with in his work as a doctor, and who now appeared before him for other reasons than physical suffering. Men he had seen suffering decisively, during a tough procedure, as he was defending their life, and who had faced their survival as though it were a task, something dependent on their will, now appeared to make requests or to launch small assaults on the almost unlimited funds generated by the Party.

Some of the men had evolved from wearing the physiognomy of suffering—a physiognomy that Lenz, in spite of everything, had learned to respect—to wearing the physiognomy of a beggar or whore, someone who for a little change will look at you like a virgin twenty times a night.

This change, this diversion of strength, this existence that heaped together completely different men in a single pit out of which emerged only living hands apparently asking for coins, these were strange diversions and detours, and almost impossible to explain. It seemed to Lenz that men liked this mysterious process of disappearing into a mass of people, and he was stunned by the official who—right in front of politician Lenz Buchmann—asked for some contribution, with a shrug of the shoulders, implicitly saying: *I'm just like all the other men.* In such a situation, the man's complete lack of shame surprised Lenz. How was it possible?

3

What do you see when you look where everyone is looking?

Lenz Buchmann retained in his mind the rare memory of himself as a child surrounded by excited crowds. Once, his father Frederich had taken him to see the military parade, and had refused to lift him up above his head or even put him on his shoulders: the child Lenz had to fight for himself in order to see. And the feeling of the child Lenz in those moments was one of pure terror, amid hundreds and hundreds of unknown legs and—more than this—legs whose attention was directed outward, the legs of hypnotized men waiting for the parade to pass so things could return to normal—so they could, that is, return to their individual concerns. In these situations the child Lenz was very afraid, not of any man in particular but of that false union, stretching from one end of the crowd to the other; a union not between one man and another man standing beside him but of two men, apart—in that moment even more brutally separated than they are in everyday life—who have come together in common admiration of the same view. People who have become allies, but not allies in the same activity: rather, in the same passivity.

Lenz Buchmann knew men; most of them became friends because they happen to share a particular shelter; only a minority—of whom he knew he was one—made friends with those who shared the same *weapon*, even if this wasn't one made of metal. And this connection was quite unusual, and far more resilient, Lenz knew—yet it was the only one that came close to the relationship of common blood that exists between a father and son, distant from contractual relationships, those logical relationships that are scattered in such large quantities across the world of the city.

4

Strategy and anatomy

This multitude, entire battalions of spectators, unarmed, had struck fear into Lenz when he was six years old, and struck fear into him now, when out the window of his office he saw common people passing by, in their hundreds, down there, passing by one another, tiny-sized; but people who, straining his eyes, he could still make out and recognize individually.

Ultimately, that high window of his was at the perfect height— to the millimeter—to allow this specialization of looks, allowing this look that could see five hundred people at once and yet could also, if necessary, dive down into just one, and see that particular body as representative, amplifying it through close attention. Whoever had built those windows, positioned like that, on that floor of the concrete building, doubtless understood not only about architecture, but politics as well.

The office window of Lenz Buchmann—already an important unit of the Party—was a window for a man of action, not for a spectator. It was for someone who sees both fields of existence: the strategic and the anatomical. From that window all his compatriots could be looked upon as strangers if he didn't care to focus on them; but from that window he could also recognize an immediate relative; he could, for example, if his father were still alive, see him quite distinctly from there: recognize his physiognomy and his way of walking, with no possibility of mistaking him. He was, then, gifted with an extraordinary combination of distance and proximity, as though by chance—and such chance could only have been engineered by the great forces that governed the world—he, Lenz Buchmann, had been granted the only window for an observer who observes in order to act, the window of great lives, the window of someone who knows that he was made to influence men one by one, and yet also all of them together.

And Lenz Buchmann, that balmy afternoon, leaning up at the window, after having passed on countless errands to his secretary Julia Liegnitz—a simple sort of girl, pretty and efficient—having completed the political chores of the day, Lenz now saw people going past, in a demonstration of the vitality of the city; people walking from one side to the other, never stopping.

And then—at that moment—unable to explain why, he felt the impulse to raise his arm and make the sign of the cross. He who had made fun of that gesture dozens of times, and who later, in the days that followed, would continue to look at it with his usual distant sarcasm.

5

The sign of the cross and another mark that Lenz dreams of making

Leaning up against the window now, as though he was a priest, he made the sign of the cross over all those walking human dots, and at that moment he thought—remembering a father talking about his sons, saying "God protect you," then correcting himself with a "God protect *us*," including himself not in the individual meanness of all those people down there but in what was in spite of everything the weakness of the whole species. At that moment the awareness that he was going to die just like everyone else he saw from his window became unbearable to Lenz; someone had made a dreadful mistake, and this had marked his whole life with irrationality.

And at that moment Lenz felt as though he was being observed. He saw himself again as a priest magnanimously blessing or forgiving a multitude of believers, but who now had behind him (without noticing) another man blessing and pardoning; and that second man had another behind him; and this other, another; and so on until the end of days and of the linear space that coincides with the succession of generations that had preceded him and that would follow. Someone will make the sign of the cross over you, thought Lenz, and again the concrete image attending this thought revolted him. He thought about his father's suicide and saw him now from another angle. He had killed himself, after all, in time to avoid declining to a point of such weakness that he would be unable to refuse this final pious gesture made over him by someone else—the sign of the cross.

Never to be the prey struck down by death, an animal still breathing but only from a tiny point of existence, he thought. Lenz was a hunter, he had always taken pleasure in hunting, and he would never under any circumstances allow this hunter to be transformed into the thing being hunted.

Then he did it, made the sign of the cross again, without thinking, over those people who were down there not stopping, resembling a single group of men following the same trajectory in circles. But no, the entire population was passing by down there: he was in the center, everyone needed something from the center of the city. That's where the food was, the transportation, the women you had to pay for. The center has everything, and the only things outside the center are details—individual houses, for example. It is there, in the center, that the explosion begins.

Lenz Buchmann, however, was happier with this second sign of the cross, in which his fingers had almost touched the glass of the window. He had made the sign with his hunter's arm, not with the arm of someone about to engage in an even fight, still less of someone merely trying to survive.

Like the owner of an ox who marks the animal's flank with the sign of his ownership, so too Lenz Buchmann, before he disappears, will make this same gesture, will mark his name on the flank of the entire population. This was his destiny. He was sure of this.

Lenz began to laugh to himself at his ambition and at how early this had begun. He remembered something he used to do to amuse himself when he was a kid: he would steal dozens and dozens of train timetables and on those tables of precise numbers that controlled and conditioned—like light—the lives of thousands of people, he would write, in black, over the top, his name:

Lenz Buchmann, Lenz Buchmann, Lenz Buchmann!

6

Can we speak in private?

From that sniper's window, Lenz was sometimes surprised to recognize someone he had dealt with during his time as a doctor. And seeing this body, now diluted within this mass of bodies whose only virtue seemed to be that they occupied Lenz's field of vision, as though employed to keep his eyes busy—a group of circus clowns or contortionists—recognizing this body, then, Lenz almost regretted ever having acted upon it. And pointing with a certain disgust at a given individual, Lenz would then remark, distressed:

"I can't believe that's the man I saved."

As though the fact of having saved him "for this"—seeing him from his window surrounded by other people—was evidence of some mistake: he had saved not an individual but a substance that was now diluted and whose essential components were calmly prepared to disappear. "Water into water," Lenz Buchmann was muttering, when the Party deputy, Hamm Kestner, the man expected to be the next president, came into the room.

"My dear Buchmann, can we speak in private?"

A DIALOGUE BETWEEN TWO STRONG MEN

1

Going down toward what's left of nature

There was something in the air, that momentous feeling that precedes the forming of great alliances. Lenz Buchmann and Hamm Kestner didn't even sit down. Their handshake was vigorous, an almost solemn act that impressed Julia Liegnitz, who was still at the door waiting for any direct instructions.

"How about we walk a little while we talk?" suggested Lenz, tired of being in that closed-off room.

Julia Liegnitz, meanwhile, withdrew.

"Quite right, let's immerse ourselves in nature," said Hamm Kestner, "but let's do it quickly, while there are still some traces of it left in the city. We haven't got long!" and he laughed.

"At least there's still whatever part of nature is represented by humans," replied Lenz.

Then Kestner spoke about the citizens who, obsessed by all those little technologies that solve their immediate problems of comfort and hygiene, only get excited when some storm blows up in the sky to make them run for shelter.

"It's only then," said Kestner, "that they remember to pray and to padlock their gates."

Lenz agreed, while at the same time gesturing with his head toward the mass of people who could be seen from his window, walking, walking without stopping, from one side to the other.

"There you see a decadence operating at full strength, and which never rests, which has no Sundays," said Lenz.

2

Making their way along the city streets, and running into a madman

The two powerful men were already out on the street, though on
a different plane from the people they had lately seen out Lenz's
window. Only a distracted glance could ever confuse these two
with those other individuals; there was a conspicuous confidence
in these men, and an energy, that weren't to be seen on any of the
other faces in the crowd. Except—curiously—the madman, one
of the better-known madmen in the city, who ran into these two
men, prompting smiles in some of the other pedestrians—at the
contrast between their seriousness and then the comical speed of
the madman; it was only on the madman's face, then, that you
could see an expression totally conquered by self-admiration and
by an unshakeable confidence in his own way of seeing the world.
He was a monarch, really.

Someone in command.

And it's in this manner that the madman made his way down
the road.

The two men even turned their faces toward him, greeting him
with a slight nod. So they paid the madman more attention than

the dozens and dozens of other people they passed, people who insisted on greeting them, in an almost commercial exchange of glances—certainly these were financial transactions. The madman, then, in spite of his lack of control in relation to the world, deserved more respect than all the others, as in him the two men could at least discern a sort of personal pride, which, if not allowing him to command other men, did at least allow him not to obey them.

This madman, who for lack of economic means had long ago left the Rosenberg asylum, did not present any danger, since he had absolutely no mastery of the instruments and techniques necessary for setting other people in motion—not even language. Therefore, no duel between the madman and these two men was possible. The madman—whom everyone in the city knew by his nickname, Rafa—made his way through the streets with the certainty of one who has chosen just the right weapon for a given moment and opponent—nobody could walk alongside him, still less behind him. The invisible weapon the madman carried—and which was at the root of his arrogance and determination—was not only insensible but also incommunicable: there were no words capable of connecting his world—and his capacity for excitement—with other people's world. In this respect, he was the opposite of those two public men, those politicians, the strength of whose weapons resided precisely in the men's visibility, and in the way their power could be understood immediately by other people. Whatever else they might be hiding, the potential violence at their command demanded respect; for it to be effective, they had to show the world a face that was—yes—perhaps somewhat inscrutable, but also, at just that moment, dangerous as well.

3

The madman Rafa entertains the city

As for the madman Rafa, the break he had made, years ago, from other humans had been a rupture not only in terms of his behavior but also in his way of bringing a noun and a verb together in a sentence. Not that the way he spoke was unintelligible, actually the disorder was not in the sentence itself but in the inexplicable journey it took from some point in his head to the outside world. His physical behavior was expressed in a language that was called into question by his words—and vice versa. They weren't just two languages regarding one another in silence, unable to understand; they were two languages that cancelled one another out, that fought, each using its own weapons.

Lenz was reminded of the fundamental conflict between a pencil and an eraser: the eraser effacing what the pencil has inscribed in the outside world, casting a word or picture back into the world of the inexplicit, of the hidden, of what does not yet exist; and the pencil which then—for the second time—insists, trying to force the existence (or rather, the re-existence) of a group of marks on the paper. This almost magical reversal, this existence that ceases to exist without leaving behind a corpse or any remains—a completely blank page, after the action of the eraser, a page that, moments earlier, might have borne the most meaningful sentence in the world, or, say, the symbol of the Party, which everyone found quite striking; this retreat, so to speak—artificial, technical, and almost monstrous—had always fascinated Lenz, and just then, at this moment, the good madman Rafa seemed to epitomize this advancing and retreating. Here was someone, thought Lenz, who has the pencil in one hand and the eraser in the other, and who acts with both hands simultaneously.

It was from this, from the impossible relationship between the two actions of writing and erasing, that the indeterminate nature of the madman Rafa's behavior grew. If only he could stop doing things with one of his hands, thought Lenz, just as he and Hamm Kestner were turning their heads, curious, to see what the madman was doing—now some distance behind them—and to the evident amusement of the normal citizens that surrounded him.

4

Neither too much, nor half

What made men laugh, then, was excess. The madman caused two conditions to coexist in a situation where a normal citizen would usually have only one. This heaping up of facts, of movements, of verbal expressions, this was what really characterized the madman Rafa; and Lenz Buchmann, as well as Hamm Kestner (two men who, together, were preparing something very significant for the city), these two men were also united, in that moment, in respect for "the good madman Rafa."

Rafa lacked for nothing, he had more than he needed; while all those other people, who delayed or sped up their steps in order to be seen or greeted by Buchmann and Kestner, they had less; precisely that: less. Those people were half-men, while the madman Rafa was two men living in a single body.

And in between these two poles, in a state of balance, unique, there was only Lenz Buchmann and Hamm Kestner: because they were not half-men, nor did they exist in excess. They were men possessed of a will that first of all knew how to prepare, to bide its time, for as long as was necessary; but when it came out, into the outside world, it emerged at precisely the right intensity to do what was required of it. A decisive will, which solves the questions of material existence in just the same way that one particular number might solve an equation. Those two powerful men—and as he walked through the city, side by side with Hamm Kestner, Lenz felt himself close to a brother, he felt a real brotherhood of blood—these men weren't smuggling their most intimate wishes through the city; it was simply that these desires wouldn't appear while their muscles were still being oiled: they'd come out later, with no negotiation, no haggling. This was how they conceived of the individual: someone already in motion, a weight that is advancing, with control, intent, and great intensity.

"Doing what we want, that is the first level; the second is making other people want what we want," in the old words of father Frederich Buchmann, spoken to his youngest son Lenz on the day he turned eighteen.

At this moment of his existence, Lenz Buchmann, one of his feet firmly planted on the first level, was already raising the other up toward the second.

5

Spirits of the forest

However, that late afternoon, it was two leaders who were making their way through the city, two instruments of something higher, belonging to a hierarchy, but a hierarchy that didn't place any single human being at its highest point, something that could perhaps only be encompassed by the word "nature," and yet this name doesn't really clarify a thing. These two men, who—without saying as much—considered themselves *the spirits of the city*, knew they owed their authority not to the same sort of fidelity that architectural materials owe to human will, but to the unending rebellion of a forest against the machines that are decimating it, even if this rebellion is clandestine, secret, invisible, patient. A rebellion, furthermore, which uses the weapon of the defeated—obscurity—but uses it with the confidence of someone convinced of his eventual victory.

It was this conqueror's energy, always there beneath the tarmac of cities, that was manifest in those two prominent politicians: the one everyone was saying would be the next president of the Party, Hamm Kestner, and the one many already considered its most brilliant member: Lenz Buchmann.

The truth was that they were not, in fact, the spirits of the *city*, but *the spirits of the forest*, which had infiltrated its streets, machines, buildings. Lenz and Kestner felt that, while they shared in the technological knowledge of their fellow men—sharing, therefore, the same degree of practical civilization—they had remained undomesticated; their will was, literally, uncivilized; not civil, and so, consequently, military; the will of men who will never accept that a weapon shouldn't be used in a city as casually as a word. They belonged to that type of man for whom a ready weapon—not to mention an obvious readiness to use it at any moment—makes up a large part of what they bring to the table, when negotiations are necessary.

A foreign king, that's how Lenz Buchmann often felt, surrounded by other men. Someone who's come over from enemy lines.

And that other man, Hamm Kestner, in spite of not having come from the same tree (he was not a Buchmann), had come from the same forest. He was Lenz's brother—with the advantage that he did not bear the same surname.

6

So that no one is left out

Lenz's life, then, was advancing toward something new. The man beside him was the signpost that marked out the beginning of a new landscape. A landscape Lenz could not yet make out, but which placed him at the center of things, no longer at a simple junction between two men, but at the center of the connection between history and so many individual lives. He was approaching a place in which each decision made had the weight of a hundred thousand decisions—where each decision vibrated, with a resonance that took in everyone, that allowed for no exceptions, left no one out.

Leave no one out, that was actually how Lenz Buchmann might have defined the ambition that guides all his decisions; he wanted to make a decision that would allow for no neutrality, that would make of each unit of the world an ally or enemy. A decision to which there was no ear that could be deaf or eye be blind—everything would be wrapped up in it.

Each of his decisions would wrap the city like a blanket. That, to be clear, was what he desired. The city was an organic thing and only this man by the name of Lenz Buchmann was capable of understanding its fears, and calming them.

7

Don't look at a dangerous thing twice

Suddenly Lenz stopped, and turned around.

In spite of his thoughts, he couldn't help staring at the madman who—though now very far behind them—was still leaving a trace of *amused disorder* in his wake.

Hamm Kestner asked him why he was still looking.

"Those sorts of people appeal to me," replied Lenz Buchmann, calmly.

"You should remedy that, Lenz, my friend," said Kestner. "It's fun to watch them as a spectator, but it's dangerous to allow them to get close. Distance. Distance, and a good laugh."

Lenz nodded, but at that moment he couldn't stop himself thinking that his wife needed to meet this strange man, urgently. She will love him, thought Lenz.

Very shortly he would have to invite good old Rafa to his house.

THE PUBLIC MAN

1

The hand of Lenz Buchmann

And how Lenz Buchmann's hand had changed! The old, almost shy way he used to govern his five fingers, maintaining a certain tension in the muscles, that secret battle that took place during surgery, taut over a piece of tissue, over a small amount of the material that makes up the world—the hand, when carrying out its medical activities, well, it was always pointing downward, and now the whole population seemed to demand that it raise its head; this private hand now looked up, that's the best way to describe it.

His right hand, at this moment, was now public. And this meant something.

He now had the sense that every one of his actions was happening on a stage, though the crowd was simultaneously his audience, who could applaud or whistle, and the object of his interventions. A situation wherein the proper judge—who was undeniably himself, Lenz Buchmann—sometimes pretended to be a defendant, so that these two roles never seemed fixed: an attempt to feed the illusion of permanence, the illusion that the whole story between himself and these other individuals hadn't been decided entirely in advance. Feeding the countless smaller ambitions of the crowd, but keeping them all at an unthreatening intensity, this was one of the jobs that Lenz understood, early on, were a part of his new position.

He had learned a lot from Hamm Kestner, and in a short time, but the gradual entry of his body into a new register had been up to Lenz and Lenz alone, and only his military attitude—inherited from his family—allied to a scientific tendency to aim always at precision—inherited from his former profession—had allowed him to reach this amazing level of political effectiveness in just a few months.

2
The transfer of skills from medicine to politics

The art of the public man is something that is exercised everywhere, there are no shelters or safe harbors. Even Lenz's own family—in this case his wife—was forced to adopt this new language. Maria Buchmann even found herself obliged to understand and integrate herself into this new applied methodology of existence. And in fact she quite enjoyed meeting new people (this was clear—and something that occasionally irritated Lenz), other men, other couples.

Lenz Buchmann himself quickly cracked the new code, and seeing himself as a scientist now investigating his own habits and actions on his workbench, he understood right away that *he had to start from someplace else*, since at the moment he found himself making decisions that would aid not an organism or an existence, but—albeit only partially—the hopes and desire of each citizen. His old medical equipment had been able to detect the corruption of particular cells—a capacity that was easily transferred from that minute scale to the normal scale of the streets, and from machines to Lenz's eye. The moral and physical disorder of the common populace alarmed him in just the same *professional* way that the physical collapse of a cell used to alarm him in his hospital consultations. It was, so to speak, a shock that nonetheless didn't much involve the one being alarmed.

Lenz the doctor was well aware of how important it was to show surprise at the precise moment when you tell the patient: *you have an illness*, even if, for him, as a doctor, the phrase didn't have even a minimal effect on his existence, but was merely a repetition, a habitual phrase, a phrase that in no way altered his, as it were, sentimental economy.

This falseness was one of the rare gestures Lenz the doctor made toward the pretence of being weak, so that his patient might feel like he had company. The practical hierarchy set up between any healthy man and any sick man was—a moment later—re-established, and therefore the doctor, any doctor, wouldn't feel like he had lost anything more than a few minutes, insignificant minutes, of strength. That moment, the moment when a doctor tells his patient that he is no longer a man but someone with a serious illness, was a fraternal moment—time occasionally takes on a material quality to which we can manage to ascribe a human physiognomy—a fraternal moment during which the doctor, showing that he is just as surprised as the sick man, *pretends that they are in the same boat*. Though, actually, they aren't.

It was this uncommon skill that Lenz Buchmann also brought over from his consultations to the various kinds of political contact he might have with some citizen. A city-planning problem—a building designed with one floor too many—or the discussion of an inheritance, in which two parties were engaged in a legal battle over one square meter, any petty problem of this type was raised by Lenz Buchmann the politician to the level of separating illness from not-illness. Everyone came out of a conversation with Lenz Buchmann convinced that he was in the same boat, all set to row alongside them, when in reality Buchmann would only be in the same boat as somebody else if that somebody else was doing the rowing for him.

Lenz had long ago done away with the refuge of ingenuousness that even the most lucid people still preserved, a refuge that he had learned early on was given a strange name, a name from the Church: the Holy Spirit. No, he never got on board—he would pretend to get on board and then quickly leave the boat again, out the other side, thereby remaining always in port, in the privileged position of an observer, with his feet firmly rooted in order and not in the unpredictable waters.

3

Setting foot in a church

From the grown-up conversations he'd had with his father, far from the verbal weakness of his brother Albert, Lenz had taken the clear idea that killing off the traces of the Holy Spirit that were left in each person's body was the beginning of another existence, an existence beyond neutral territory.

Motors don't work in the swamp, Frederich Buchmann had told him on the same day that Lenz took his first communion, while he was still dressed in a way that made him feel completely idiotic, just to satisfy his mother's Christian ideas, and this expression that he heard just a few minutes from the door to the church had marked him, and over the course of his growing up, year by year, he would keep coming back to that phrase, understanding it more and more clearly.

And, early on, when he was still just thirteen, he had said to his mother, in a tone that would allow no additional words to be spoken in reply: I will never set foot in a church again.

4

The possible relationships between the body of a man and the Holy Spirit

Of course, tearing down or eliminating the Holy Spirit that one organism had put—without permission—into another wasn't as easy as just deciding never to go into a church again. Because it was really a matter of a concrete mechanism given a suggestive name: the Holy Spirit had been transformed by the philosophers of the Church into a kind of protein of the fraternity, a protein that was not human, but made rather of some other substance, with some other quality, the effect of a rationality that is perfectly humiliating to humans, but which they (thought Lenz) stupidly accepted with their empty smiles. *What in you is most worthy does not belong to you*, the Church had said, with the invention of this nonhuman Spirit that, according to Frederich Buchmann, had come to occupy a space where previously there had been nothing lacking. The Holy Spirit was an excess, a substance specializing in a function that was not indispensable to existence. It was like taking a machine that was working perfectly, according to its design, satisfying all the requirements made of its power and mobility, and then adding a second motor that runs independently but with no connection to the rest of the mechanism. That is, it's not even a piece that could replace another that breaks down: *it is an extra piece.*

Consider two men from two countries who speak only their native tongues, each one's language incomprehensible to the other, and who are locked in a room and tasked with formulating a speech. What will come out of this room will be two autonomous, independent speeches, occasionally even containing opposing propositions or explicit declarations of war; the only way to avoid this would be for one of the men to leave the room, agreeing to abandon their common ground. For Lenz, these are the possible relationships between the body of a man and this thing they call the Holy Spirit.

5

The importance of terrain to the proper functioning of things

"*Motors don't work in the swamp,*" said Lenz Buchmann to his secretary Julia Liegnitz, many years after first hearing this phrase from his father's mouth. And he said it in response to Julia Liegnitz's resistance to writing a letter to an important industrialist who wanted Lenz to do certain things for him. A letter in reply, and one that was a lie from beginning to end.

There had never been a situation like it.

It's true that very early on it had become quite clear that the relationship between Lenz Buchmann and the citizens of the city wasn't built around truth, but around whatever part of truth might make it possible for his name to acquire solidity and renown. Now, however, in this situation, greater courage was required: Buchmann had given an order to Julia Liegnitz to write sentences directly in opposition to the truth: to stand facing a white wall and declare that the wall is black, or to know full well that the following day is Tuesday and yet to state that it is not, and swear it too, if necessary.

Of course, Julia Liegnitz wouldn't dare refuse the task assigned to her, but her discomfort about this explicit sacrificing of the truth, and then—the immediate effect of the foregoing—her discomfort about sacrificing the idea she held about herself as a person who would not deliberately lie—at least not in situations where she wasn't emotionally involved—this discomfort was so explicit (and yet another aspect of her ingenuousness was to be found in this display) that Lenz Buchmann had no choice but to set out, in an almost uncivilized fashion—which did give him some pleasure—the doctrine of his relations with the world.

And Julia listened.

6
We don't fish, we sink boats

"Go to any church you want, girl, I'd even advise it." Thus did Lenz Buchmann conclude a long conversation. "I even think your presence might be important there, representing my peaceful intentions toward that extraordinary institution. Please, don't miss a single Sunday."

The Church, thought Lenz, was not one of mankind's natural allies: it was one of those groups from which we demand only a well-behaved muteness; their weapons only weaken our own arsenal, *we are from another Kingdom, and it's no good walking on water if you hope to impress people in your political career.*

The followers of Buchmann and Kestner came from other stock, they weren't fishermen: *the people who follow us will only be impressed when they see the boats of our enemies sunk, one by one.*

The truth was, the price of anarchy had fallen in recent years. The places from which it could be fomented were cheap and plentiful. Such was the confusion, and so many the cries of grocers proud to be founding a new religion, inventing a new machine, or, simply, a new arrangement of their garden, that everyone, tired of the growing multiplicity of voices, now awaited not new inventions but a return to the old order, the old condition of existence, in short to the time when there had been only one position, a position guarded with the most modern of weapons and commanded by the most indomitable of voices.

Lenz knew that if he and the other members of the Party were to decide to cut off the electricity supply, while guaranteeing the security of each individual fully and continuously, instead of intermittently, like they did now, it wouldn't be long before *we would have them again—the populace,* said Lenz, *holding candles, proud that these will allow them to attend nighttime military parades to watch those protecting their goods and children parading past.*

Everyone wanted security, but first they wanted to feel more threatened.

THE LIEGNITZES AND THE BUCHMANNS

1

Links that are not cut

From the very beginning Lenz Buchmann had respected that woman, Julia Liegnitz, for reasons of blood that only he knew. It had been his father who had opened up the decisive crack in that family. So it was his mission, in the restoring of a dignity whose rules were defined by him alone, to continue the work of his father, Frederich. It was essentially the same action, but disguised: to protect that woman and the whole Liegnitz family—especially her brother, Gustav Liegnitz—was interfering in their lives, in the way that only a superior member of the hierarchy can interfere—just as his father had done. Essentially, Lenz Buchmann was positioning himself on a plane where, as far as their existences were concerned, killing and protecting had begun to resemble one another.

He felt duty bound to protect the children of the soldier his father had killed, through a desire to redress an injustice, yes, but also with the pride of someone following his father's path, passed down like a legacy—an inheritance, in this case, occupying a psychological rather than physical space. In any case, the reasons weren't what mattered; the truth was that these two families—the

Buchmanns occupying the superior position and the Liegnitzes the more common one, the inferior—had been linked, bound together, by a deed of great intensity, and this link had to be respected by the generations that followed. It was respect, then, that Lenz Buchmann was showing when he ignored the theft, indisputably committed by his secretary, of a certain sum of money—thus winning from Julia an absolute fidelity—and also when, over several years, he took on the task of teaching the mechanisms of existence to Julia Liegnitz.

2

Julia learns to write properly

So it was with an almost paternal pride that he later saw the smile of understanding from the Liegnitz girl at the end of his first political text, which she had drafted herself, and in which he had clearly lied.

And he was more satisfied still, later, when he witnessed the gradual dilution over time of that spy's or smuggler's smile of hers, because this dilution meant that lying had earned a new status in the public life of Julia Liegnitz. It was no longer something that set off her conscience, but a professional task, an office activity that one does more or less efficiently, which has been perfected or not, but which never causes shock or even has any significance. She had learned to remove the motor from the swamp.

With each day that passed Lenz Buchmann felt a stronger bond with this girl, Julia Liegnitz. He was making her, in a sense, *doing her* as in times gone by he had done the little servant girl at his parents' house. A violation that was not sexual, but which was continuous—not grabbing hold of someone only to let them go again afterward, but grabbing hold and never letting go; first destroying, crushing, turning shapeless, bringing all their old values down to the same level, which then, yes, begins to give them a new shape, enabling Lenz to infiltrate and lead with a new strength. Day by day, the woman was abandoning her ingenuousness completely.

In two years, the politician Lenz Buchmann and his secretary Julia Liegnitz became inseparable. Like in the process of osmosis: a single substance.

THE NAMES

1

Two names that have gained in strength over centuries prepare themselves for a duel

At the very beginning of their professional relationship, Lenz Buchmann expressed his desire to meet his secretary's brother: Gustav Liegnitz. The repetition of the name he had first heard from his own father—Frederich—resounded like a significant historical fact; the name represented another kind of monument, not a material one but of equal symbolic importance.

Certain names are actually things—that is, constructions that deserved to be visited in just the same way as a centuries-old church. Sometimes Lenz almost considered the possibility of a universal tourist circuit; tourists who don't want to learn the history of stones of or swords broken on battlefields, but who are curious about the energy—indeterminate in nature—that you feel when you hear a powerful name.

It was quite clear to Lenz that alphabetical order had become a monstrous thing. There was a inherent connection between names, a kind of vibration, an excitement that always infiltrated this overly civilized order; like someone willing to take dangerous short-cuts in order to find his brother all the more quickly, certain names always ran ahead, in search of others. A family name concentrated a group of ancient experiences that could never just be thrown into a basket and counted like pieces of fruit: individual experiences aren't units. They aren't a matter—as Lenz had learned from his father—of an operation along the lines of 1 + 1 + 1.

Adding sums is a pitiful operation compared to what becomes visible at the moment that you hear—just for example—the name Buchmann. Alphabets and balance sheets aren't capable of holding this force that a single word can contain—words are like warehouses, holding successive concentrations of experiences from different generations, experiences that always occupy the same space (if we can think of a name in that way—as a space, a certain set of square meters). Names, therefore, become more and more dense; with every generation that passes, a family name accumulates greater density within the same limited space. Thus, from generation to generation, the danger of an explosion increases as the forces expand to occupy a smaller and smaller area.

Lenz felt that even a name had a limit to its capacity as a warehouse or a hiding place. And if the name Buchmann was a storage space where more experiences were still being accumulated, the name Liegnitz was too. Increasingly concentrated forces occupied decreasing space, packed away not to disappear, but to attack, later—after gathering its strength—when least expected, striking the most effective blow.

It was this feeling of devotion toward family names, this conviction that any one of these names was more than just a neutral word, like *chair* or *table*, but precisely a word opposed to all neutrality, an unyielding word, unique, not to be confused with any other—it was this feeling that led Lenz to wish for, and at the same time fear, a meeting with Julia's brother, Gustav Liegnitz, since he had exactly the same name as his father . . . and this fact alone was enough to make Lenz aware that the history between their two families was not yet over. The final shot hasn't been fired, he thought. Though it did also seem to him extremely unlikely that anything resembling what had happened in the past would happen again.

But a name, a given name and a family name, repeated in a later generation, is not only a tribute to something that no longer exists (or something that, in principle, is expected to stop existing before the name is reused), it's also a public demonstration that the work goes on—in each generation the family name seeks the best possible position on the battlefield. A position it might pass on, once more—but which was never definitive. Combat—whatever form it took—always postponed the ultimate decision, and the technical end of this historic energy would at last be indicated simply by the end of a family name.

2

The alphabet as a way of flattening the world

Lenz so respected the history of every name that he was repelled each time he saw the word *Buchmann* in its place—the letter *B*—on any huge list, as though it was no more than that: a word beginning with a particular letter.

In this alphabetical ordering he saw what was, all told, an attempt to replace ancient forces with anarchy. It meant, really, that there was no order, no rational beginning. No tower is ever positioned in such a way that only the first orders are issued from there. Everything became leveled, a machine being led perhaps by a drunk man had cancelled out all the differences of height (and not only these) between new buildings, fifteen-century-old ruins, well-kept gardens, forests still unowned, men and women, children and old people, deficients, lunatics, beggars, rich men, horses and lizards, tables, chairs, books, various pieces of music: everything had been flattened and the world thought of as though it were all composed of a single material, in which differences were imagined only to give things an order, making everything seem to make sense,

names and their precedence according to the alphabet all perfectly comprehensible.

Lenz Buchmann was not, however, prepared to live in a squashed,
flat world.

DANGER UNDER THE GROUND

1
What you fear can emerge from anywhere

With his father Frederich Buchmann he had in the past visited the ruins of edifices from centuries past and in them had detected a dangerous grandeur and a strength he rarely saw in modern buildings, built and held up with the latest technologies. In the middle of the ruins there was still a mysterious force circulating.

The ruins are dangerous, Frederich Buchmann used to say to his sons Albert and Lenz; *they still have something moving underneath.*

This image marked many of Lenz's nightmares. He grew up convinced that there was another world, not that of the heights—which lay beyond his field of vision—but a subterranean one—threateningly below his feet—and which, as such, was located in a privileged position. Every military strategy stated the obvious: take the enemy from behind, face to face only when you're the more powerful, and from above, of course—whoever is on top has the advantage, hence all these tall ramparts in the world, as everyone knows—yet no reference is ever made to an enemy coming from below: attack *from below* is never considered.

The firm ground and black earth were impenetrable, places where human combat had no place. It was above the earth that combat happened, and could happen at different altitudes and according to thousands of strategies. However, *under the ground* had always remained the great mystery to Lenz—and at the same time the great fear: since he recognized men's inability to descend to that battlefield, so unlike the relative ease with which—for example—they can go into the sea.

He had also noticed—and this was obvious whenever he visited some ruins—that it was not neutral ground: the final strength of nature lived there, the force that the civilization of the city had not yet been able to tame. And more than just a mysterious armory, the underground was the inverted tower out of which emerged—or could emerge at any moment—the next great orders, the next great law. Humanity had not yet struck a blow at the true enemy's word of command.

If men were sensible they wouldn't allow a single stone, a single trace of the previous centuries to remain, thought Lenz—ruins were dangerous. Under them—underneath, that is, the failure of a construction—a space was formed that encouraged the development of a cruelty for which men had no words, and—worse than this—against which they had no defense.

Human cruelty, civilized cruelty, always makes a shield for itself that might very well be formed from the same material with which it comes under attack by other human cruelties. . . it wouldn't shock Lenz at all to discover that the sword and shield of two enemies could have come, not only from the same workshop, but from the same piece of metal, from the same steel. Or, in other words, from the same force. The force is split into two and one part defends us, the other attacks us.

However, about *uncivilized cruelty*, the cruelty for which no possible alphabetical order can exist, about this underground cruelty, nothing was known: there weren't any tools for shaping or unshaping it to our tastes, as yet. The cruelty of nature, which had its territory in the earth under ruins, hard and yet humid enough for growth, was still being developed. It was still a child, this cruelty. When it reaches adulthood, then, thought Lenz, yes, then it will be our great enemy.

Lenz Buchmann, let us say, considered some men—though, yes, only a few—to be his adversaries. That is, he saw them as being in possession of weapons fashioned from the same piece of metal as his own. And yet, he never felt threatened as he had done as a child when visiting the ruins of what his father Frederich had explained had been an old torture chamber.

There was nothing to fear from anything above the ground. The remnants of one instrument of torture or other had provoked only laughter in the two children. Those remnants seemed like toys now.

All the fear came from below, from what he, his brother, and even his father, were unable to see. And that was precisely the main cause of the fear: they couldn't see it.

Lenz Buchmann liked being alive, he was even proud of his violent and uncompromising way of taking possession of his days— and even of other people's days—but at certain moments he did get the sense that something was eluding him, that he was playing the wrong game or in a battle where he was defending or attempting to conquer lands he had no real interest in. At such moments he felt like there was no direction—really none at all—that was barred to the weapon he held in his hand. He could fire at anything, just like an attack on him could come from anywhere.

THE MEETING WITH GUSTAV LIEGNITZ

1

A sudden burst of laughter

The date for Lenz Buchmann to meet Gustav Liegnitz had been set.

Lenz was prepared for anything. He knew there was no way the Liegnitz family could suspect what had happened in the war between Frederich Buchmann and Gustav Liegnitz senior, but Lenz didn't only respect clear facts—he knew as well that certain catastrophes were born from forces that develop in secret. Indeed, Lenz thought these non-visible movements might resemble the gestures a person could make, facing someone else, with one hand behind his back: a hand shockingly visible to himself—albeit not to his eyes—but invisible to this other person standing right in front of him.

For Lenz, historical facts, history in its broadest sense, besides its visible face, also constituted a series of these behind-the-back movements. However, because we are (hypnotized) in front of history's visible events, we don't notice these others. Which was precisely what had happened in this particular instance. The Liegnitz family wasn't aware of what had really happened—that too had been done behind their backs—but this didn't mean there weren't always instincts, intuitions. Lenz wasn't afraid, but this all meant he did feel a tense respect for Julia Liegnitz's brother.

The daughter, thought Lenz, grows in order to give continuity to the family, while it's the son who grows—gaining strength—to avenge the father. The daughter grows to build, the son to destroy.

The son of the soldier Gustav Liegnitz was therefore a potential enemy. If he—the son of soldier Gustav—knew how to read the non-visible writing left in the air by the meeting between their two fathers, he would quickly propose a duel and straightaway pick up his gun.

That meeting was the historic synthesis of many events from across the generations. Strengths and weaknesses that had mixed together to form this Buchmann part and that Liegnitz part—the latter a family that, to Lenz's mind, had acquired a borrowed and unexpected grandeur due entirely to the episode that had brought it into contact with his own.

That episode which had taken place in the previous generation endowed the son of Liegnitz with an uncommon authority: he was a man who had historic legitimacy for being Lenz's adversary. He was a man with a right, which far superseded the law: *the right to vengeance.*

"My brother is different," Julia Liegnitz had tried to say, but Lenz asked her not to go on.

"I want to meet him," said Lenz, "don't tell me about him."

When Lenz Buchmann got up to greet his secretary's brother who had just come into his office led by her hand, his reaction was so extremely indelicate that it was fortunate nobody fully noticed it: Buchmann gave an involuntary laugh. Gustav Liegnitz was a deaf-mute, who made a few shapeless *mmms*, and, Julia explained, heard all sounds as muffled. (Gustav Liegnitz wasn't even able to speak the name Buchmann.) This, thought Lenz, could never be my adversary.

ANOTHER DIALOGUE BETWEEN BUCHMANN AND KESTNER

1

The broken bond

The two of them were walking along the city's busiest streets as they had done so many times lately. It was on the move that they worked out their political strategies. Without saying as much explicitly, the two men had intuitively assumed that all their significant conversations would take place while walking: walking, always walking. And there was a kind of faith: the impetus of their muscular movements, going through a more or less mysterious translation of energy, would be transferred into their words. Words spoken while taking some sort of action immediately convey signs of impatience, which was essential to the beginning of any significant event. Lenz Buchmann and Hamm Kestner understood one another perfectly, undertaking both of these movements: walking and thinking.

"We are surrounded by cowards," said Kestner all of a sudden.

According to Kestner, the city was beginning to feel closer to death than to life. He had the feeling that the masses, if given their freedom, wouldn't storm any palaces; they would run for cover. What any revolution needed now was more security, not more power.

Ever since the moment—said Kestner—when understanding and dialogue had replaced the old instinct for justice that marked certain agglomerations of human beings, since the moment when criminals began to get attentive hearings from assemblies of their peers, when secretaries were assigned to note down carefully all of a killer's arguments, ever since the moment when the nearest trees and the strongest ropes had ceased providing an immediate implementation (right there at the scene of the crime) of the people's verdict, from then on there was nothing left to fear.

Kestner gave a smile. Lenz remained impassive. Their ideas were entirely congruent. Kestner was of an exceptional bluntness—that is, he was not ingenuous, and he didn't play games with his words in order to feign ingenuousness. Lenz Buchmann liked that kind of man, of whom there were fewer and fewer around. Besides this, the two of them had imbibed fully of certain of the more violent arguments that were circulating the world in those days.

At this point, Lenz said:

"My father often told me that the bond that used to join the population to the old kings has long since been broken. Now what we find between the two parties, more than fear, is indifference."

A leader, thought Lenz, could order the beheading of one member of each family, or invite the entire city to a dance, and the reaction would be more or less the same.

2
Fleeing to the Bastille to get out of the rain

The dialogue continued. Kestner said that the question was who had broken that bond, that material thing which linked spectators to their spectacle. Now history (Kestner went on) was passing before these people's eyes, and they didn't even notice it. They wave at great events like a baby in a crib, said Lenz.

Which was why the Party had urgent work ahead.

"We have to arrange a kind of ceremony," said Lenz, "in which the two pieces of the puzzle are brought back together."

The thing was, this problem of passivity worked both ways: on the one hand it stopped the cretins from taking the Bastille again (Lenz said this out loud to Kestner), and with their so primitive hands controlling machines that they cannot master, but it also (said Lenz, bluntly) stops them from listening to us. They are deaf and dumb, which is not good if we want to have a conversation with them (he concluded).

"We can simply give them orders, we don't have to have a conversation," Kestner commented.

Indifference was a dangerous thing. In the short term it could have its uses, but with time it would become even more threatening than another powerful Party, argued Lenz. It was a total, ludicrous indifference: no one challenged a single law any more.

"If only we could just start the species again from scratch," said Kestner.

A REFLECTION

1

Losing everything: losing reason, losing control

Lenz paid particular attention to the idea that man, besides being a repository of books, of science, of techniques, of tools (and he was an example of this), also had over the course of the centuries learned *to be a better animal,* to be more effective as a bearer of organic necessities and instincts, in whom rationality was not the key characteristic. It was, he thought, as though beyond human culture man had actually constructed a second history, that of the culture of the species. And this part of the evolution of man was also a journey that could allow a generation to be more effective than the generation that preceded it.

Between him and his father, Frederich: could it be that Lenz was *more cultured* in relation to his hunger, that he was possessed of a greater capacity for directing his sexual excitement?

Obviously, he didn't know much about the secrets of his father's life with his mother or with other women—doubtless there had existed, as there had with Lenz, a second narrative, a narrative running parallel to the marriage—and, knowing nothing about this second life, he couldn't draw any kind of comparison.

However, Lenz did detect—it was quite apparent in himself—the lack of control that sexual excitement provoked in him. Everything Lenz was able to do, when sexually aroused, belonged to a group of actions that could never entirely bear his name, precisely because there was a dislocation of the ownership of his body. Lenz felt, then, that he was borrowing his limbs and his vitality from a force that ran parallel to his will and which did not have a single point in common with his rationality and intelligence—the reasons for many people's admiration of him. What he did when he was sexually aroused, his need to be watched, his approaches to a certain type of person who clearly was not a part of his physical or mental world—crude men or women, prostitutes, beggars, and even madmen, like that Rafa, about whom he had often thought lately—what he did in those moments *when things went beyond him* was not in truth a *doing*, but the opposite: *it was something being* done to *him*. At such moments (which could last just a few minutes, the time it took for his sperm to be expelled) he felt himself to be something being shaped, a material that fragilely accepts the form that some force wants to impose on it.

It was clear as well that this dilution of his will—this state in which he was unable to make his own decisions—later provoked an uncontrollable revulsion in him. All the people who had ever participated in these moments were looked upon by Lenz—a minute after their final consummation—with the same disgust as he had felt when looking at his first corpse, unmade by a bomb; an uncontrollable, muscular disgust, which went beyond the world of causes and effects completely, beyond the world of charts and calculations, the world of sentences, the library world he had inherited from his father; and he entered this other grotesque universe, stripped of all explanations, where a dog was growling at a child because the child was afraid, where a wolf was stopping still with an enormous tension building up in its legs, not because it was about to launch an attack but because its feces was about to come out; this immediate, material world where the ground that seems solid actually swallows up a man's whole shoe and foot, this was the second world that Lenz felt himself entering when aroused: a world he could neither control nor understand.

He was disgusted at the surprise that these uncontrolled parts of the world provoked in his body, and as such he looked at the excitement and moral disorder and—more serious still—the *rational* disorder that existed in him at these moments in the same way as he looked out a window at a storm. A lightning flash was an event as strange to Lenz's will as the acts he performed when aroused.

The disgust he then felt was not so much moral in itself as attributable to his obsession for control. He despised people who took part in these moments of disorder—his own wife and the strange men he drew into the roles of observer or participant—since they were complicit in the assault on his own will: his wife and the others participated in a revolt that—albeit temporarily—rescinded his power over other people.

Apart from the fact that the physical and psychological coercion was his, in the moments after the consummation of his excitement Lenz looked at the participants and felt himself to be someone who obeyed, not someone who had just given the orders.

When Lenz kicked the tramp out after—in front of him—having had sex with his wife, he did this out of shame. Not shame at the lack of some moral value or other, but for the lack of strength it revealed. He was someone who knew that his power over others depended on the fact of his maintaining a permanent grip on an object, and yet, even so, at certain moments (and with no obligation to do so), he found himself putting it down.

When aroused he put down his reason and made his way over to the other side, obeying.

TAKING HOLD OF THE INTERIOR OF THE LAW WITHOUT BURNING YOUR FINGERS

1

Give me one reason not to kill the weak

In spite of the great casualness that he tried to convey—exhibiting an uncommon ease in his contact with even the most wretched elements of the city—Lenz did not stop feeling embarrassed, even threatened, when he was out on the street and came across the tramp with whom he had signed a kind of secret contract, providing a generous donation in exchange for the man's taking up his position as observer of a couple's sexual act.

More than an encounter with any political rival or a chance meeting with a former medical colleague who at the time had been even more highly esteemed than he himself, Lenz definitely felt at such times as though he was suddenly in the middle of a duel, facing off against the tramp—the weakest part of the city.

Sometimes, in what were periods of reduced desire or when he forgot the usefulness of that tramp, Lenz thought that the way of solving this problem—the uncomfortable feeling he felt every time they met—was to get rid of the man entirely. And really, it wouldn't be difficult.

Lenz almost smiled at the thought of the striking disproportion between the danger inherent in ordering a man like that killed, a man without any relations, without any significant connections (this man had no one to whom he could say *good morning!* at the beginning of the day), and the danger—yes, a real, intense danger—in conspiring against the life of the current president of the Party, or of his powerful friend Kestner.

All men lived under the same law, and the city and each of its inhabitants took pride in this. However, it was evident that the most important law, the fundamental law, was not the law on paper that tried to create a balance between two men. There was a practical hierarchy that utterly defeated the theoretical hierarchy that laws tried to impose. And actually, the problem with laws, to Lenz, was precisely that: they did not impose, they argued. The laws of the city, in peacetime, had replaced orders with arguments, as though ultimately a good conversation were enough to convince a rapist to go to prison for six years or a murderer to undergo the death penalty, of his own accord, leaving home in the morning and arriving punctually at the firing-squad wall.

Lenz did not belong to this world. The evident facility with which he could order the killing of a poor beggar or that good madman Rafa, surely without this having any consequences for him—he would still get the same good-mornings from the citizens—led him to a fierce loathing for the idea of law.

Lenz couldn't help thinking that even in the most equitable societies, in what appeared to be the fairest societies, powerful men only didn't kill a tramp, right there in the street, in front of everyone else, with their bare hands or with a weapon, because they didn't want to humiliate the country's laws in public, since they themselves were, in some respects, the guardians of those laws.

DESIRE

1
And an indisposition

Lenz Buchmann smiled, took a cigarette from his pocket and lit it.

Obviously desire was beginning to interfere with his thoughts—
a stain, at once pleasant and unpleasant, beginning to grow.

It had already been a few uneventful weeks now.

He looked at his watch, trying to distance himself from the
headaches that had insisted on assailing him lately. What was
going on?

He remembered that he had some appointment to go to, but it
had become quite unimportant. Right now he couldn't even recall
what it was. He was on another plane, now. On another level.

He got up. *Nothing to be done*, muttered Lenz Buchmann to
himself. *Nothing to be done.*

At that moment it was no longer him who had mastery over
his head.

He was thinking about his wife and about Rafa, the madman.
Right now it was the madman who was giving the orders in Dr.
Lenz's head.

SOME EXTREMELY BRIEF CONSIDERATIONS ON GUSTAV LIEGNITZ

1

Not even a deaf-mute is always lovable

After his first meeting with the important politician Lenz Buchmann, his sister Julia's immediate superior, Gustav Liegnitz saw his life change radically. Owing to Buchmann's particular influence, he was not only given a job suitable to his physical condition, and very well paid to boot, but he also rose two positions at once, completely breaking with the rigorously regulated system of promotions within the structure he had just entered.

The fact that he was being protected quite explicitly—there was nothing camouflaged about it—by the important Dr. Buchmann (there had even been one or two visits to his workplace) also led to a complete overhaul of his relationships with other people.

Gustav Liegnitz had no very special qualities. Deaf-mute from birth, the youngest son of a soldier who "died in combat," and who (fortunately, some said, because of his son's deficiencies) never got to see him. And apart from the usual compassion for someone who was deaf-mute, he'd never received any other strong displays of affection over the years. In fact, until the great change—the break—that the meeting with Lenz Buchmann had instigated and defined, young Liegnitz had been classified as lazy, not particularly intelligent, and of poor character.

As someone who was extremely mistrustful of the usual day-to-day requests made of him, he became obscenely subservient in the presence of someone powerful. These poor qualities, among others, were however quickly dissolved when the change took place in young Liegnitz's life. He was now publicly under the protection of the man people were already talking about as a possible vice president of the Party, in the event that his friend and ally Hamm Kestner won the elections.

And so he moved naturally into a period during which people would comment among themselves: "Interesting how young Liegnitz, in spite of that problem of his, managed to develop such a capacity for hard work." People said things like that, banal things.

However, this period passed within a few months. And the evil eye over him returned.

Now Gustav Liegnitz's ill-nature was revealed in another way, expressed from a position of strength rather than his former position of weakness. His character was even more visible, and even more significant. The young Gustav Liegnitz, a deaf-mute from birth, protected by Lenz Buchmann, became more and more unbearable to his colleagues at work with each day that passed.

There was something else about the deaf-mute Gustav Liegnitz, which was little known: he was quite ambitious. If he could have spoken, this would have been obvious to people long ago. But no.

THE MADMAN SHOWS UP IN THE WRONG PLACE

1
Morning, at Party headquarters

An episode that disturbed the operations of the Party, albeit with no other, greater consequence.

Lenz Buchmann was sitting at his desk, in that stretch of time that he sometimes kept only for himself, reading. Some shouting began to disturb him, however. He lowered his book just as his secretary, Julia Liegnitz, opened the office door.

"I'm sorry, Doctor. It's that madman, Rafa. He says he wants to speak to you. He says he's your friend. That Mr. Buchmann had said he wanted to talk to him. He's downstairs and he's yelling."

"Tell him to come up. Yes, yes, that's right. Don't make that face. Tell him to come up, come up. Yes, I want to talk to him. What are you thinking? What's all this nonsense? Tell him to come in and put a stop to all that commotion. And then close the door for me. I want to be alone with the man."

Julia Liegnitz remained silent for a few seconds. Then she spoke.

"There's no way we can tell him to come up. Mr. Kestner already called the police. They're downstairs."

2

It's better to watch from above than to be dragged down

"Lenz, how many times have I told you to drop it? How can a man like that possibly come into our building? Keep away from those people."

This almost insignificant episode had visibly annoyed Lenz's friend and ally Hamm Kestner.

Lenz replied:

"You agreed that people like this Rafa inspire more confidence than most people you see around."

"Let's drop the fairy tales," Kestner interrupted, "we know one another well enough now. I know you're attracted to these people, and it has nothing to do with your fine political heart, my dear friend, we both know that. It's something very intense and personal. I'm not getting involved in your private affairs, you can do what you like, but not here. This isn't good for either of us. I need you, Buchmann. Please don't do anything stupid—think about us, and about those people who lower their voices as soon as they see you pass. Don't throw away everything you've already achieved. They're even saying that you've been giving significant sums of money to that brother and sister, the Liegnitzes. That doesn't sound good to me. People are already talking about it. They insinuate that you're having an affair with the girl Julia. We have to maintain some dignity, Lenz."

Lenz got up.

"I'm not having any kind of affair with the Liegnitz girl. I wouldn't dare do such a thing. And we've said all there was to say, Kestner, my friend. Don't trouble yourself any further. I've listened carefully to you. I'll follow your advice. Don't worry. I know we both want the same thing. Let's move on."

But let's say, in any case, that the rumor that Julia was Lenz's lover really was completely unfounded. It's true that a few months after his young secretary had begun her job Lenz Buchmann had tried a little something, which would no doubt be followed by several others. But Julia Liegnitz, with the delicacy that characterized her, and giving the impression she hadn't noticed, very courteously halted his advances. And that, definitively, was that. Mere rumors, then.

As for the madman, he was taken away from that place, as he had to be. It was the headquarters of the Party.

SIGNS OF THE APPEARANCE OF A NEW CIVILIZATION

1

Don't listen to what the priests say

Critical elections were approaching, and the departure of the old president of the Party created a sudden appetite in several men. Not all of them, however, were starting from positions of equal opportunity.

In the city, Lenz Buchmann was no longer a unit on whom people placed bets—on how long he would last, on how far his influence might spread. He had left behind the insubstantiality of accidents or apparitions. He would still be around in a few months' time, not just a name in people's memories. Lenz was already the famous bearer of one of those right hands that seek to destroy in order to recreate in their own unique way; and as number two to the leading candidate, Hamm Kestner, he had already taken control of the (non-physical) arsenal at his disposal, provoking fear and imposing respect. In sum, Lenz's presence excited individual attention. One by one, each man, as the important politician passed, brought his feet together, and made himself as compact as possible, tensing the muscles in his back—assuming the stance of a soldier not in wartime.

It should be noted that Buchmann brought about this state of attention not on Kestner's behalf but on his own, thanks to his brilliance of mind and the way he combined a practical authority with an ethos that was expressed in powerful formulations. It was Lenz who had come up with the founding statement of Kestner's campaign: "Movement must be forced." This "forced movement" quickly became a kind of password, moving from man to man.

The incumbent city government remained focused exclusively on developing space, fascinated by square meters and by what could be built on them. In this context, Buchmann was able to propose the idea that merely filling up space is for cowards— movement was the important thing. For the moment, it was a matter of toppling the idea that construction upward was what best characterized the century.

For Lenz, construction upward was a kind of capitulation. Contrary to what many people argued, Lenz said that man already knew the sky. The Church-born instinct to continue to elevate ourselves higher than anyone had ever managed, and which had never been able to protect anyone from any actual catastrophe, this instinct had contaminated the city, which now rose instead of advancing. The fact that he believed that moving vertically was not an advance, that one only advanced *close to the ground*, led Buchmann to classify movement and velocity as the greatest assets of the masses. Thus *the other side*, about which the masses are naturally curious, should be moved away from those unknown, magical places—"the afterlife," "heaven," "hell"—toward what actually exists, the proof of whose existence is the fact that they can be knocked down. Whatever cannot be knocked down doesn't exist, Buchmann argued, and as for churches, it's a fact that they do exist. But *let us leave them be,* he said: *they have weapons that they only fire after we speak up.* As for God, He couldn't be knocked down. Hence his power.

And we're not just talking about a building, the Church wasn't built by men stupid enough as to say "this building is our God." They knew perfectly well that a building from a century that doesn't have the technology to knock it down yet will only end up being knocked down by the better-aimed weapons of the next. But men would never be able to knock down a building that hasn't even been built. That, to Lenz, was the trick of it.

However, Lenz Buchmann knew how to read the traces of civilization, just as he had learned to read the tracks that his quarry left behind it in the forest. He had understood early on that the system of credit that the city had constructed around God was beginning to run out. The most sensible citizens had already stopped lending even their spare change to someone who had never paid them back for what, generations earlier, they had left in his charge—in a kind of moral savings account that they had thought they might be able to make use of later on.

It wasn't hard to work out whom they would prefer now, thinking of them as an army, if they were given their choice of leaders, allowed to decide who would speak the word of command, a priest or a good military strategist. Even if the general was a monster; even if, individually, every one of his soldiers was afraid to be left alone with him; even—indeed—if this strategist was known as an out-and-out crook, everyone would feel safer under the auspices of his words. The words of a priest in this context would only make them laugh.

2

Not the whole: an arm of the world

Frederich Buchmann had passed on to his son the idea that the greatest life was only to be found in places and times where there was nothing but the need to kill in order not to be killed. The need to kill, just as in other times and places a citizen at peace has an absolute need for food or sleep. With the act of killing having become a necessity, not merely one choice out of many, humanity stood (according to Frederich Buchmann) with its most universal—and least specialized—reason revealed.

In fact, Lenz Buchmann had recently shocked a devotee of the Church by telling him—not in the tone of someone trying to shock, but like someone passing on a piece of almost pointless information to a guest who's just arrived—that the soul about which the Church was always speaking was something that only specialists could understand and see; these specialists (said Lenz) we call believers, the most respected title of all, at a moral level. It didn't stop, however, being the question of a technical detail; really, the soul was just something that concerned this new profession—the believer—and didn't have anything to do with moral questions as some were claiming. In which case (Buchmann went on in the same provocative tone), this element, which is only recognized and manipulated by specialists, is a specific object, something that doesn't enclose everything else. It's made of only a part of the world—like a man who only has one arm, or even like an amputated arm we see at the side of the road.

Whereas, thought Lenz, everything else in the world participates in the same instinctive movement, the movement of survival, of personal, private resistance: animals, too, and even a plant, which might seem calm above the surface and indifferent to its own destiny but is burrowing obsessively under the earth in the search for water or the best position for its topmost part to receive enough light. Everything has this universal instinct, which is not the property of any one profession and isn't surrounded by believers, precisely because it's impossible for the category of nonbeliever to exist, in this context, argued Lenz. All are involved, all have been called.

It is this that is the great breath that ran and still runs through the world: defend yourself, kill if necessary, do anything to survive; no possibility is excluded, all actions are possible, and all actions are good as long as they meet their objective.

3

Specialists scared by a universalist

Your soul is for specialists—Buchmann repeated to one of the priests who was simply stupefied at the way this powerful man spoke.

Buchmann was well aware that he needed the priests; he had, however, understood the basis for mastering them. The strategy was simple: make them afraid, these priests, when alone with them. One man—Lenz Buchmann—faced with a priest, with no witnesses and on ground considered sacred by the Church—that's the ideal scenario; it was crucial that the threat be made on the other's turf, so that the other understands whose side is stronger.

Fear is what mobilizes, fear is what makes the only universal instinct visible, which leaves no one out and about which it's possible to say that nothing exists that isn't (or doesn't want to be) turned toward it—recalling the way certain plants seek the best position to get light; in this case, a black light. Fear demands a commitment from all organic things, a repositioning, an attention, a preparation for the decisive movement.

And the priest—another one, in front of him now—was already mobilized, mobilized on behalf of Lenz Buchmann's great political idea, an idea that formed the basis of the whole campaign for Kestner, the candidate for the presidency of the Party.

So it was with great pleasure that at the end of what the priest considered "a fruitful dialogue," the man took Lenz's hand and said, "You can count on me, I'll use all the influence I can."

It wasn't just a matter of having mobilized an enemy to fight in Lenz's own trenches, albeit with the recruit's own weapon—that is, a weapon still bearing the insignia of his old allegiance. In a manner far more reliable than any contract—because he had done it out of fear—the enemy had agreed to be Lenz's ally. An important victory in the Party's campaign.

4

The importance of electricity

Strictly speaking, Buchmann and Kestner—Kestner himself—did not see the Church and the priests as their enemies.

The Church no longer had the strength it used to have. Its sacred stones, which the Church's publicity materials claimed still bore the incorruptible energy of the first days, had long been covered in cloths made by new technologies, fabrics made not to last a century but to glow intensely for just a few months.

The Church had transformed itself—or had allowed itself to be transformed by the world—into just one more association, which the country already had not in the hundreds but in the thousands.

Men had always had a weakness for association, for coming together, in a simulation of actual wartime, when the association of forces isn't born from some theoretical formulation—a collection of statutes—but from a sense that some immediate necessity (or imminent death) is placing before their eyes a test that cannot be overcome individually. And if the Church has members—and just like any group of people, some of these do nothing but fulfill their formal obligations, while others confuse their lives with the group's projects—so too the Association of Firemen or the Association of Lawyers have theirs; and even old soldiers have their own association, perhaps out of a kind of nostalgia for those great gatherings of death, which is what all real battles are.

The Church was only a partial mobilizer, and if it happened to resist, its resistance didn't amount to much, like any other insignificant association. If all the believers—or even the priests themselves—went on strike, this would be far less noteworthy or visible an event than a strike by plumbers or electricians. The efficient distribution of water and electricity had become far more indispensable to day-to-day life than the efficient distribution of the divine breath.

5

The role of children

Lenz Buchmann had already spoken on this subject with Kestner: the Church really wasn't an element worth fighting. Nor was an alliance with them critical. There was a wall in the world, whose position and height allowed decisive men—men like Buchmann and Kestner—to climb up and there obtain a better vantage point from which to watch, or to shoot.

So what, then, was the Church to these two strong men? A child, expendable, whom the sniper asks for help, just so that it doesn't feel left out. The child, pleased just to be useful (in the Church's case, thanks to its long history, one might add a "still" here too), brings his hands together for the shooter to rest his foot in, to get his balance as he climbs up. A few seconds up there, supported by this enormous effort on the child's part, will be enough for the good marksman, on top of the wall, to aim and fire.

"My friend," said Buchmann, at the end of one of his several visits to a church, "I look on you as a son. I respect you as one."

The priest thanked him, bowing down, a private humiliation that Buchmann knew was a far more precious investment than any public one, however tempting.

"We're on the same side," the two men said at that moment, shaking hands.

And they were, they were on the same side; but Buchmann wasn't the one playing the part of the child.

HOW DO YOU HUNT BIG GAME?

1

Distance and competence

Lenz Buchmann, who had been born with the most lucid of genes, had later learned through medicine to keep a certain distance from other men's suffering, a distance that people might classify as *an incapacity for empathy*, or even as *perversity*; or, alternatively, could simply be understood as pure professionalism.

Sentiment ought not to rust the scalpel, according to Lenz, who believed that competence was exercised from an objective point of view and that this point of view presupposed a certain distancing; a gap between the object to be saved (or about to die) and its savior (or its executioner). Excessive closeness was a sign of professional incompetence—this is what Buchmann had taught his young trainees when he was a doctor. However, what he didn't say at the time—and had now gained the courage to say—was that excessive closeness was also a sign of *moral* incompetence. A doctor can only act well if he has achieved some distance from the suffering of the sick man; to act well—to act morally—is to act competently.

A doctor filled with fine feelings, but with a right hand that shakes, is not a good doctor, and not a good man; he is someone who, his whole life, will be cursed by the relatives of the patient whose body suffered the effects of *an incompetent detour of his scalpel.*

.

2
In praise of slowness

In the long conversations between Lenz Buchmann and Hamm Kestner, the question of how to mobilize the city became a decisive one. When Lenz came up with the expression *forced movement*, he immediately clarified two presuppositions: without feeling real fear, men would never be mobilized in significant numbers; and once they *had* been mobilized, it would be necessary for there to be something still pursuing them, something that never stops. The hard thing, said Lenz, is conveying to each man the feeling that— even if he is squeezed into a little cell—he has control over the entire world.

From the book that was his guide for a good part of his life, and which he had inherited from his father's library, Lenz Buchmann retained the line that—as much in his work as a doctor as in his work as a politician—came to define his behavior, and which had disturbed him from the very first: "Fear is the mystery that speed conceals."

What was interesting was that these words had structured his profession as a doctor in a different, indeed opposite way from

that in which they now seemed to apply to his political thinking. As a doctor—and, in particular, at the moment of his surgical
interventions—what he heard in those words, "fear is the mystery
that speed conceals," was the absolute need to impose slowness on
all his professional movements.

Intervening in an organism's most minute tissues, the scalpel
seeming to touch them cell by cell—being someone who takes a
blade and cuts away the black tissue from the rest—is a task that
requires unlimited patience, a slowness that can go so far as to be
confused, from an outside perspective, with absolute immobility.
And in a sense, when in the past Dr. Lenz was operating, he did
indeed do so from a position of immobility, an immobility that
ultimately changed its position imperceptibly.

To Lenz Buchmann, the competent surgeon, in his time working on *individual tasks*, speed was actually an enemy. A surgeon
was only quick if he was afraid; he only wants to get it over with
if he doesn't have absolute confidence in what he's doing, if he's
afraid of making a mistake.

Very early he had understood that—even with inertia—it was
far easier to set something in motion than to manage to keep that
thing in motion from stopping.

But things were different now, and Lenz Buchmann's tasks were
no longer *one to one*. As he moved in the opposite direction, he
had attained an unusual breadth—of acting *one-to-many*—and as
the months passed those *many* increased in number and that *one*
concentrated himself around a single point, with the uncommon
intensity that comes from having one single objective. Step by
step Lenz felt the extremities of his ambition drop off, the outside

edges. Those "distant relatives," those lesser projects or thoughts, had been abandoned by Buchmann, and his central mass had been becoming more and more densely focused around his one idea: gaining more power by forcing people into motion.

Circumstances had changed completely, but the importance of those words—"fear is the mystery that speed conceals"—remained; focused, now, on the actions of others.

3

Not for now

Deferment was, *par excellence*, the word of power, the word of the king who with a thumbs-down can condemn a prisoner to death, but who at the last minute decides to defer this gesture. He isn't having second thoughts—but he's going to think about it. It is only a *not yet*—or, the most dreadful deferment of all, *not for now*.

This *not for now*, Lenz well knew, had a greater reach than simple, definitive execution; it could keep an entire city under your control.

If—with Kestner—Buchmann won the Party elections, he would then have the necessary authority, as vice president, to use the *not for now* anywhere in the city. There would be no shelter or refuge impervious to those words, if they came from Lenz Buchmann, he thought; and he would say as much to Julia Liegnitz, with whom he was building a complicit trust that far outstripped the simple contractual relationship he had with the woman.

To be a man with the power to say *not for now*; this was the position Lenz Buchmann wanted to conquer.

4

Two fears

What most shocked Buchmann was the way that fear and speed mixed together after a certain point, making it impossible to tell them apart. He was already looking at a new substance—like the hydrogen and oxygen in a molecule of water—a substance (fear/ speed) that was more explosive than dynamite.

Or perhaps, to be more precise: it was the great fuse of the world, as this mixture was not itself the explosion but the trajectory that would end in a great explosion. Buchmann would say to Kestner in their conversations about strategy: the more we manage to infect the population with this mixture, rapid movement and fear, the stronger we'll be. Never letting them stop so that they never stop being afraid. Never allowing them to stop being afraid so that they never stop.

There needed to be two fears, then, not only one. The first fear to get things started, get them moving out of their immobility; the second, more powerful fear would keep things in motion. When ten thousand inhabitants, belonging to a certain ethnic group, unprotected and made up almost entirely of old people, women, and children, began to flee their homes upon receiving the terrible news that some other group was advancing upon them, when this happened, this first movement of abandoning the land of their birth was motivated by the first fear. However, what made these refugees—after two hundred kilometers on foot—keep on moving, as quickly as possible, forgetting the weakest among them and those who are beginning to fade, what made this happen, two hundred kilometers later, was the second fear, the more powerful one, which keeps in motion what has already been in motion now for a long time. This second fear is so strong that is makes it possible to defeat the limits of fatigue: night will fall, but none of them will want to rest.

5

The example of the hunt

While on this subject, Lenz was reminded of his time hunting. When a hare sensed him and began its flight, moving from an unconcerned immobility to a hurtling race, crude and disordered, then, in that first moment, the hare was being invaded by the first form of terror. A good hunter—and he, Lenz Buchmann, was proud to be one—did not give up on the hare after this first flight. A good hunter would go on, at a slow pace, without too much rush (the slowness of a careful step, guiding one's boots well, that's what defines a good hunter), slowly, every footstep considered, always transmitting the information that he is in charge of the situation, a feeling that one way or another will be received by the quarry. A good hunter proceeds in this way, and with just two or three of his well-placed steps in the middle of the forest he will be able to instill the second fear in the fleeing hare, the decisive fear. And it will be out of this fear that the hare will really begin to hurry, to race off at full speed, but a speed without order or objective, recalling those little mice locked in cages that run inside of wheels, turning them with their feet;

movements that are very quick indeed, but in a category of motion that might be described as *the speed of someone just trying to keep going,* so different from *the speed of someone who wants to advance.*

It was only when—in his role as hunter—he realized that he could strike this second fear into the hare that Lenz Buchmann became completely convinced that the animal would not escape him. His many years' hunting had taught him that this second terror—unlike the first—has only detrimental effects for the quarry: it is illogical, almost suicidal. The first fear, being instinctive, makes the quarry flee in a direction away from the hunter—any intelligent living creature would do that. The second fear, however, once it invades the organism being pursued, completely disorders the strategic system that all living creatures have, and can bring the quarry around in a circular route ending up—stupidly—five meters from the hunter's weapon.

And this was the real meaning of forcing things into motion. Forced movement, movement provoked by fear, was an extra movement, removing all possibility of control, disordering an organism's concept of its position and orientation, and allowing the word of command to do what it pleases with the creature in flight.

That moment, shall we say, the moment when the hare stupidly comes to a stop right in front of him, is the moment of the true hunter. It is a tiny length of time—just an instant—but if the hunter can predict when it will come, he will find the thing he's been hunting for right there in front of him: the hunter's position has evolved from one of attack to one of execution; his weapon already raised, the hare there in front of him, and then—the well-aimed shot. Once again, the hunter uses to his advantage the terrible mystery that whoever is being pursued carries at their core.

That's how to deal with hares, thought Lenz, and that's how to deal with people.

6

One more warning to be ignored

At that moment Lenz Buchmann was alone, in the Party office, and he smiled.

All his life up to that point, all the tasks he had carried out at a professional level, even on Sundays, which other people used for lazing around, seemed now to make sense; a single sense, which came together in the centre of his organism and waited, like a silent, unmoving predator getting ready to pounce. Or just waited, like the words *not for now* wait, gathering strength.

Yes, Lenz Buchmann waited, but he didn't want to maintain this state of deferment for ever. Buchmann was anxious for the moment when—faced with the expectations of a huge crowd— he would (slowly, aware of the practical consequences) turn his thumb downward, like the ancient kings used to do.

Everything in the outside world advanced as he predicted it would. And Lenz Buchmann's position in the world would be perfect—were it not for the tremendous headaches that now attacked him, insistently, from someplace; a place that was his, certainly, but over which he had no control.

In spite of this, of these terribly strong headaches, in spite of this warning, Lenz Buchmann still remained preoccupied with the mechanisms of his weaponry and the demarcation of his targets.

SPECTATORS AND SPECTACLE

1

How many are standing beside you?

What fascinated Lenz about unusual people, led astray by their own steps or else driven out by others, was the absolute personal freedom with which they made their choices. In a madman or a beggar who wandered the streets asking for bread and soup, and who at night only wanted—just like any other human being—to get some sleep, Buchmann saw someone who could make choices in absolute freedom, and without consequences, possessed of his own individual morality. A morality that doesn't have a single peer, a single secondary element to go with it.

Who would challenge the "immoral life" of a beggar or a madman? Those men already carry within themselves—because of their difference—a burden of immorality that is universal and profound, and which makes them immune to the practice of other, little immoralities.

A madman—just like a beggar—is not immoral. Madmen are individuals, there can be no imitations, rather like a king; a person without peer, who doesn't ever have *someone alongside them*. Which is why, for these expelled men—just like the most powerful men—there can be no criteria for comparison with the rest of humanity.

Buchmann looked admiringly at those men who carried their own system of laws with them in their pockets, signed with their own names.

In a sense, this was what Buchmann desired: to bear a legal system whose laws applied only to him; to bear a morality that isn't that of the civilized world, nor that of the primitive world; which isn't the morality of the city or even the morality of his own family but a morality that bears his name, his alone.

2

Whom do you choose for a spectator?

Our intimate instincts that separate good from evil—or, more specifically, that define our personal, private, internal legal systems— aren't something that it's possible to share.

As far as other people went, it was only Lenz's father who'd ever had an inborn morality that Lenz felt he could commune with— and commune with it he did, with the same degree of determination—even when there was no one watching—that he had invested into all the other aspects of his life.

And in this regard, Buchmann had understood very early that for most people, individual morality—the legal system within a single citizen—was only ever revealed when there was no one watching them. When there are spectators the prevailing morality is diluted and tries to express itself using the values of those present—a game of seduction, like a bad actor trying to entrance an audience. This is the world of the common man and its banal spectators; it was a world to which Buchmann did not want to belong.

The great quality those madmen and tramps had was precisely the fact that they always acted as though they had no spectators, as though they were alone in the world. And they really were. They weren't loved, they did not love, they weren't hated: their terrain was free, allowing them to be free.

And free men excited Lenz Buchmann. This made them the ideal spectators, too.

In recent days he hadn't been able to keep the image of the madman Rafa from infiltrating his thoughts. That man was attractive to Lenz. In him, he could sense the possibility of finding his own great spectator, being as he was undeniably the one great free man of the city.

The city, of course, had no need of free men, but Lenz Buchmann's personal life increasingly demanded this exciting freedom; a freedom so free that it sees everything and judges nothing. Only sees, sees.

Lenz Buchmann, let us say, sometimes felt—and his intense headaches were also a part of this feeling—as though he had less control over his own organism than over the city, and this made him at once proud and afraid.

But at that moment, this was what mattered: it was only with those sorts of spectator—*those cast adrift*—that he, Lenz Buchmann, could be absolutely immoral. A unique individual, with no imitations.

He needed them, then.

A TRAGIC OCCURRENCE

1
The spectator raises his head

It should be obvious that Lenz Buchmann was never going to stop before he reached the point of utter immorality: and now the madman Rafa had just walked into his house. He was standing there, in his kitchen, and, strangely, not very talkative. He'd accepted Lenz's invitation and now there he was: so what do they want with him?

Buchmann had already called his wife, introduced her to Rafa, as he had done the first time with the tramp. Maria Buchmann gave a big smile.

"My wife, Maria," said Buchmann. "This is Rafa, a good friend."

Then there was the whole building up of a feeling of control, be it over his wife or over these strangers he had invited to visit, the city's rejects. To begin with, on the whole, conversations were utterly pointless, but with this man—Rafa—conversation was even more irrelevant than usual. An exchange of perfectly disconnected phrases, accompanied by wine, and observed from the outside, from a distance, by his wife, who scarcely said a word, but who from time to time smiled at her husband, with a look so explicit that to Lenz it seemed like that of a prostitute, one who happened to have the uncommon particularity of bearing his name—Buchmann. His wife was a Buchmann prostitute: excellent, he thought sardonically.

By this time, however, impatience generally had the upper hand, had become the most powerful element. And so it was. Lenz, excited, started touching his wife while the madman—unlike what had happened with that beggar who had visited them so frequently—never lowered his gaze. On the contrary, he was watching, explicitly, *with no humility at all*, watching Lenz's hand on his wife's breast; and more than this, he made a comment, out loud, about *what Dr. Lenz was doing to his wife*.

It was as though the three people present—including Lenz himself—could see nothing and needed this assistance: a madman describing each of his movements.

Buchmann felt that sense of strangeness which pleased him so much. This change in the attitude of his observer had completely dislocated the situation, as it were, but it kept Lenz excited. The madman didn't lower his gaze, he used words and common expressions and laughed at what Lenz and his wife were starting to do.

Lenz asked his wife to get up, and right there, on the table, with just a chair between the madman and them, he began to lift up her skirt, at the same time as he was unbuttoning his trousers. The madman Rafa didn't leave off with his obscenities, but he suddenly got up and with an impressive shove threw Lenz Buchmann to the ground, while at the same time shouting, unrestrained, that he was going to be the one, the one to do it, saying: "Let me be the one to do it, Doctor!" as though the two men were accomplices, as he grabbed Mrs. Buchmann hard.

Then Lenz got up quickly and took his hunting rifle down off the wall. Without any hesitation at all, he cocked it.

Mrs. Buchmann tried to defend herself against the madman. He was forcing her to keep her back toward him, pushing her head down violently, and from the fly of his trousers he had already taken his stiff penis.

Then there was a bang. Lenz fired a well-aimed shot into the head of the good madman Rafa.

For a moment, Lenz Buchmann just stood there, the weapon in position. His hands firm, unmoving. His wife already had her panties halfway down her thighs, revealing her very red buttocks.

Then something went through Lenz Buchmann's mind. "Fear is the mystery that speed conceals"? Yes, perhaps it was that. But how can we know?

It was quick, Lenz moved the barrel of the gun just a few centimeters, pointed it at the head of Mrs. Buchmann, and fired again.

2

The news reaches the city

The whole city was stunned when the news spread.

The way it was told was as follows: a madman—Rafa—had gone into the house of well-known politician Lenz Buchmann with the intent of robbing him, and having been caught in flagrante, he took Dr. Buchmann's hunting rifle and shot Mrs. Buchmann, killing her. After a struggle, Dr. Buchmann retrieved the weapon and managed to bring Rafa down, just as he was trying to escape. Such is the story recorded in the police files and subsequently by history.

Needless to say, some of Lenz Buchmann's strange behavior had already been widely discussed, and many people weren't convinced that the madman Rafa's entry into the house wasn't by invitation from the owner of the house.

Lenz Buchmann's little perversion had prompted comments for years now, though it would never have passed through anybody's head that the rest of the story might be equally untrue. Even those people who allowed themselves a little ironic smile over the insinuations regarding "the madman's too-easy entry into a well-guarded house" would have thought it unacceptable to presume that the respected Dr. Lenz Buchmann, one of the potential leaders of the city, might have killed his wife.

Besides the natural protection that his important name gave him, Lenz Buchmann had been extremely careful. In the very same moment, without any pause from which thought and reason might create a thread of cause and effect, Lenz had put down the gun and tried to arrange the bodies in a position that corresponded logically to the only story that could clear him.

He arranged the panties of his wife—Mrs. Buchmann—with great difficulty, since with the impact of the bullet her body had fallen face down; and he also rearranged her skirt so as to eliminate completely any trace of a sexual advance. Then, within the same intensity of the moment, at *the same speed*, in a sort of fever that kept his body completely contained within those urgent minutes, Lenz leaned over Rafa and—dispelling his disgust by the speed with which he did it—pushed the madman's penis back into his trousers, then pulling his zipper up, as though nothing had happened. He then moved the body away to a position that seemed to him the most appropriate.

When the police arrived, they were like that, two bodies with their heads broken apart—the shots had been discharged at very close range—bodies that had tumbled onto the kitchen floor of the house of Dr. Lenz Buchmann, who—with uncommon courage—recounted all the details of the incident. The first time still inside the space of the tragedy, the second in front of the most eminent police officer in the city, who with his solicitous gestures first invited Lenz to sit in a chair and then, before asking him any questions, said in a tone of such subservience that Lenz had to struggle not to laugh:

"I'm so very sorry, Mr. Buchmann, I'm so very sorry. These things just aren't . . . It's a disaster, Mr. Buchmann, a disaster."

EVEN MORE STRENGTH—AN EXPLOSION AT THE THEATER

1

Manufacturing danger, but not industrializing it

Lenz Buchmann and Hamm Kestner had already spoken about the possibility of an explosion in the building of the city's largest theater, a *possibly necessary* means of establishing a state of tension in the city. That first fear, which would come in useful to the Party.

It was only possible to wipe out tedium with localized explosions, one explosion close to each individual, an explosion for every citizen, said Buchmann to Kestner, amused.

The two of them had found a new direction for their campaign—a secret direction, of course: to manufacture a danger that they themselves would subsequently defeat. Without a sense of constant danger there could be no heroes, and these two men didn't want to win their authority by vote alone; they knew that the authority of the old concepts of courage and strength were the only things that could withstand the fluctuations provoked by a number of incidents. Buchmann and Kestner would seem to be the only people capable of confronting a terror whose origin had not yet been identified.

It was a serious matter: Buchmann and Kestner wanted to win the elections. It wasn't a game in which each player agrees to play with only the permitted number of cards in his hand. It was crucial to begin with the principle that the other side just didn't have the right methods to fulfill their aims. An opponent is always working toward an objective, and this object demands certain means, which in peacetime are no more than weapons in disguise. Who could fight such an arsenal with their bare hands and a predictable strategy? Neither side were children. Buchmann and Kestner's opponents were gentlemen with out-of-date ideas, but they too came from a tradition of fighting: in a direct confrontation there was nothing they wouldn't do. Then, however, yes, then they would accept the result.

It was obvious, however, that Buchmann and Kestner *overall* were more exciting than their opponents *overall*. It was the difference between someone quoting an old saying and someone coining a new one that will be repeated by the generations to come. Buchmann and Kestner were on a higher plane, a level from which it's possible for an individual to take a great leap.

They had a group of unquantifiable forces at their disposal. They had simplified their ideas and as a result there were no obstacles to their morality of action. First, create a danger whose origin couldn't be identified; then, through this, force the population into movement; finally, prepare the ideal, strong state from which two types of people will emerge: those who protect and those who are protected. These were the tasks that were laid out on the table of Kestner and Buchmann's world. With fewer tasks than there were fingers on their right hands, everything was quite simple.

The two men had made their decision: a small explosion would take place close to the main theater. It wouldn't hurt anyone, Kestner argued; and Buchmann agreed.

2

The first fear; learn it in the forest, apply it in the city

Processes do not always run according to plan; in this deliberately modest explosion, one man died. The bomb had been placed in a side entrance of the theater, in a small room where there was a statue of an old king, an unconditional supporter of the theater in his time. The statue was shattered, which allowed both Kestner and Buchmann's side and its opponents to argue publicly and vigorously for a common project: "The reconstruction of the statue, at double the size, to be put on display in a more prominent and noble place inside the theater." A statue that would never really be constructed.

A minor actor had died in the explosion, his name unknown to the public; he happened by mischance to be passing the place at the wrong time. The tributes "to the great actor" who had died at that moment "of great responsibility for the city," since "the existence of a real danger" now showed the vital need for a strong leader of the Party— these tributes did appear, like new explosive bursts, but now kindly ones, from the same bomb; and all distinguished men attended the funeral, which was even more popular than (and indeed completely extinguished the emotion that only three weeks earlier had been provoked by) the funeral of Mrs. Maria Buchmann.

That private tragedy had been followed by a public tragedy, threatening every person in the city. The difference between a weapon with a single barrel firing a single bullet—like the voice of a teacher who calls a boy by name and thus gives him permission to rise from his chair—and a bomb that doesn't even know the name of "his pupils" was clear to see: chaos and the lack of sense or explanation to justify the violence were effective ways of sweeping away any sense of security in the city. Buchmann and Kestner knew this very well.

No one took responsibility for the bomb; no one understood its causes. Only this much became clear: the explosion hadn't been meant for that poor actor. And so: it could have been meant for anyone. And so fear was established. The first fear.

EVEN HIGHER

1

The library gains in strength

Cleared of the penal consequences of having killed the madman Rafa thanks to acting "provably in legitimate self-defense," Lenz Buchmann not only didn't see any damage to his reputation but, quite the contrary, saw himself acquiring the human dimension of "someone who has suffered terribly." If his former hardness and conviction had won many men over to his side, this occurrence—which demonstrated that even Lenz was susceptible to being struck by these dangerous times—won over the female public. If he had planned some strategy of this kind—to win over both halves of the public—it couldn't have been more effective.

With the private tragedy that had struck him, Buchmann became far and away the most talked about and most highly respected man in the city. Not only did he already have power, and not only was he poised to win it in—as it were—a technical way, via the Party elections, he had also already suffered what naïve people considered a violent defeat: the death, and under such circumstances, of his wife.

Without having calculated it, Buchmann had managed something that not even a hundred thousand concrete political acts could have produced: conquering the fear instinct as well as—at the same time—the instinct for compassion in others. Who could hope to stand against someone who has shown himself all the more powerful after having suffered? This was the question that—on a nonverbal level—filtered through the city and led to every public appearance by Buchmann being surrounded by a bestial hubbub, which went on for a long while after the eminent man had already disappeared back into the most important and influential buildings through doors that were inaccessible to common citizens.

Every place Lenz went was being transformed into offices and every man he met becoming an element within a common construction for which only he, Lenz Buchmann, seemed to have the final plans. He no longer had any doubt: it would be thanks to him, Lenz, that Kestner would win the elections. His father Frederich Buchmann could be proud: his son was in the world of the strong, and in that world he was free. He had freed himself of a woman whom he now saw, clearly, had been utterly common, and in that sense had been a companion who had sabotaged his every moment, slowing the speed of his step; and he was free, too, of the erroneous manifestation of the Buchmann name that had been his brother Albert.

The family library, meanwhile, considered now as a whole, had been growing at an unusual pace. There were few contemporary authors who didn't send Lenz their books, and some of these were incorporated into the main part of the library, since Lenz could see in these books the strong new impulse that pleased him and that seemed to be coming up in the world.

2

While you're looking the other way, blows to the head

And so his name was clean. Now there was one single Buchmann, and this man was about to become one of the most important men in the city, if not the most important of all.

It was the big night, election night, and Lenz Buchmann and Hamm Kestner and a few people close to them—including Lenz's secretary, the Liegnitz girl—were waiting for the final result of "the voice of the people." Kestner was joking around, though a little nervous, and Lenz too was more unsettled and less confident than usual.

In Lenz's case this wasn't because of any fear that they might lose the election, they were going to win, he was quite sure of that. His discomfort was not external, but caused by his intense head-aches, which wouldn't go away. A few days earlier, the pains—about which he complained only to Julia Liegnitz—seemed to have leaped up to another level, seeking to attract the full atten-tion of their owner—a common dog biting its master so that he gives it some notice.

The need to carry out certain activities before election day meant that Buchmann had paid no attention to the pain—which was now almost constant—and simply placed it onto the tray from which he recently seemed to be displaying his heart to every little crowd he wanted to conquer. The game of *large-number* seduction in which he had become involved prevented him from confronting his own individual body in the way that had once been second nature, in part due to his former activities as a doctor. This diminishing of self-vigilance, leading him into the role of someone in a permanent mode of attack, would end that night.

There was no longer anything to do: they could only wait for the results. And perhaps due to this sudden reduction in aggression, Buchmann at last allowed his body to express itself. He began to size up the headaches he was feeling.

They were actually uncommonly intense, excessive, even brutal.

3
Victory incomplete

The news they were waiting for arrived at the end of the night: Hamm Kestner had won the elections. So Lenz Buchmann was now—formally—the second most powerful man in the Party, and once he had finally resolved the question of these headaches that were pursuing him, he could carry on with his project in peace.

He was well aware that if his father were alive he would never, at any point, whatever it might be, have been prepared to allow a pause in his advance. Lenz Buchmann's position in the world was—on the night of their victory in the election—that of a combatant who agrees to rest because the previous days have been hard; however, some traces of whatever enemy still existed remained now in his body. That night, like no other night, was at most the armistice that precedes the most violent nights of all.

In the middle of the city's central square, standing beside his ally and new president, Hamm Kestner, he received hugs and greetings and thanked in return former classmates, old doctors, ladies, and old men, some of whom repeated stories countless times about his father Frederich; and in spite of the pains in his head, unbearable, he stayed quite late, in the middle of the party, as he was its center, there was no doubt about that—Kestner was merely Lenz's future adversary.

A strong man, certainly, without scruples, and allied to that kind of intelligent violence that Lenz also recognized in himself, but Kestner was not invincible, far from it. Nor was he a friend, either.

Lenz Buchmann said good-bye, then, to the new president of the Party, with a strong hug, hailed enthusiastically by the crowds; but returning home, accompanied by his secretary Julia Liegnitz, struggling not to be overwhelmed by the pains in his head, which threatened to become uncontrollable at any moment, he muttered to the Liegnitz girl:

"He's not going to be keeping that job long. I'm going to kill him."

DIAGNOSIS OF THE ILLNESS

1

Looking at the same thing in a different way

"I've seen pictures like this before countless times," said Lenz Buchmann, irritated, as he held the X-rays of his head in his hands.

"Yes, Mr. Buchmann . . ." said the doctor, "but now it's your own head."

"That doesn't scare me!" said Buchmann.

"There's nothing we can do. The only thing . . ."

"Don't interrupt me," said Lenz. "I wasn't finished."

"I'm sorry, Dr. Buchmann."

Lenz pulled the X-rays back over toward him and looked at them carefully. It was unmistakable. The black spots were everywhere. His head was already no longer entirely his. It had been invaded, from inside, cravenly.

What, then, should he say in this situation? This is something Lenz Buchmann had never learned.

PART TWO

ILLNESS

WAKING UP SURROUNDED BY MACHINERY AND BEING GRATEFUL

1

The hand loses weight

Surrounded by tubes that at first sight and at first feeling seemed to be emerging from the inside of his own body, and not coming from outside, and surrounded as well by various other bits of mechanical equipment, with red and green lights signaling states that at first glance no one would be able to interpret too precisely, Lenz Buchmann awakes, still half-dazed, in the hospital bed, several hours after the operation on his head. He doesn't immediately understand where he is nor what is happening to him, and his only impulse comes from some occurrence that he locates—vaguely— toward the right side of his body. Foggy to begin with, the thing then gains in definition: someone is stealing his right hand from him, or at least that is what he thinks at this moment. He cranes his neck slightly, still finding it hard because of the pain, and sees a woman, his secretary Julia Liegnitz, with her two hands on his right hand, his powerful right hand that suddenly seems dead to him, an autonomous corpse that has not yet been separated. In order to confirm one way or the other, Lenz makes an effort to move its fingers and no, no, it's not dead; the fingers move. Then he contracts—just a bit—the palm of the hand. The hand has maintained function, the muscles still retain their powers of contraction and relaxation intact.

But what has happened to his hand? It's gone soft—he can't find any other expression—as it lies under Julia's hands, just like any other useless bulk. He tries to raise it, without warning, to get it away from that state of humiliation; then, however, he does run into resistance: the movement would have to begin from the muscles of his shoulder if he means to lift his entire arm, or at least from the area around the elbow. But he can't do it; he doesn't have the strength to lift his arm and pull his hand away from Julia's. He doesn't have the strength.

Julia says something, and he hears it as though his ear were also just waking up, its full capacities not yet restored. He doesn't understand what Julia is saying, perhaps words like, *Rest, don't worry.*

"I can't lift my hand," mutters Lenz Buchmann, his voice all muddled.

And at that moment he can hear clearly.

"Dr. Lenz, leave your hand. I've got it."

Dr. Lenz Buchmann hadn't even made it into the new quarters to which the vice president of the city is entitled. The doctors observing him decided not to wait so much as an hour. Lenz Buchmann had a tumor in his head, and it was already very well developed. He was awaking now from general anesthetic after an operation that had been long, very delicate, and inconclusive. The illness had already spread; it had been on the move for a long time. They had performed an operation, reduced the area occupied by the enemy, but there was a lot of it left to be defeated. The "thing" was already advancing into other organs.

For the doctors who had operated, it was obvious that all that was left now was to wait. Death was right there.

"My head hurts," said Lenz, with no idea that the illness had long ceased being satisfied with just the top part of his body.

A NEW BODY RETURNS TO A NEW HOUSE

1
Intimate changes

Weeks later Lenz Buchmann left hospital on his own two feet. He had, apparently, recovered his energy.

Beside him, but not needing to help him, were Julia and her deaf-mute brother, who repeated an *mmm* that—trying to be caring—irritated Lenz profoundly.

"Enough with the *mmm*s," Lenz even said at this point, rudely.

Gustav Liegnitz helped wherever was necessary, but it was Julia who managed and organized everything.

Julia had positioned herself at the center of operations.

By now she was a fully-made woman, who knew the world and the different stages through which each organism passed. She had grown up without a father, and her mother had disappeared years earlier, too. From a very early age, she had protected her brother whose deficiency made him an easy target for children's mockery. Mockery and sarcasm, which would later be exchanged for a much more polite difficulty in finding work—*What's a deaf-mute going to do? He's still got his eyes. But what's he going to do with them? Watch?*

It was Julia who got him his first job, and if it hadn't been for that encounter with the powerful Dr. Lenz Buchmann and the resulting vertiginous professional ascent of Gustav Liegnitz, Julia would doubtless still be hovering around her brother, alert to his needs, ready to defend him, as though the two of them were still at playtime in primary school, surrounded by children making fun of his shapeless *mmm*s.

One could say that Gustav Liegnitz did speak a little. His *mmm*s were really an attempt to sketch words out, to sound out letters; an attempt that his sister—after years of practiced listening—now managed to discern almost perfectly. Julia often functioned as a sort of translator for her brother.

One might also say that, when he concentrated, Gustav Liegnitz could make out what a person's lips were saying. He couldn't hear, but it was as though he could see the words forming, right there, at their source. He saw the sculpting—so to speak—of the words—he didn't hear them.

Gustav Liegnitz wasn't stupid—quite the contrary. His intellectual faculties weren't brilliant, certainly, but quite normal, *average*. The difficulty was always overcoming the prejudice according to which anyone unable to speak—like children—must surely be infantile, or infantilized, as far their learning, their intelligence. And it was not without some surprise that people discovered that Gustav Liegnitz knew how to write. It was as though they were witnessing a piece of magic: a deaf-mute writing—how it is possible? This ignorance of his abilities—which were perfectly normal in every respect save speech and hearing—was, in short, the greatest obstacle that needed overcoming in Gustav Liegnitz's life.

In any case, the circumstances of the Liezgnitz siblings had again changed dramatically in recent days.

With Lenz Buchmann's illness now acknowledged, and following his operation, first one Liegnitz and then the other took the final step toward intimacy with the still powerful Buchmann.

2

Two new tenants come to help

Since the death of his wife, Lenz had lived alone. So it was quite natural that the Liegnitz siblings should move into the big Buchmann house—Julia ostensibly in her capacity as secretary, but with each week that passed moving further into the role of nurse, someone who helps not with a body's professional life but with the body itself.

Gustav Liegnitz, in turn, gradually took over the running of the household, and more specifically of the small investments belonging to Buchmann family, or what was left of it—that is, Lenz alone.

Thus, Lenz Buchmann's physical decline was accompanied by the advent of an ever more forceful presence, a force that imposed itself on every square meter of his house—the two Liegnitz siblings. In short, the Liegnitz family was advancing.

In other circumstances, and seen from a distance, this sequence of events, the flagrant occupation of Buchmann territory on the part of the Liegnitz family, might have seemed like an invasion, a conquest. It was all happening, however, with an uncommon harmony.

Lenz Buchmann, who had walked himself out of hospital, vigorous, didn't retain that vigor for very many days. A little more than two weeks later, after three visits to his new office and one conversation with the powerful, recently elected president of the Party, Hamm Kestner, he decided to stay away from—as it were—the public part of the city.

He realized that his physical weakness was widely known. He was the target of other men's looks (he always had been), but the looks were now quite different. They were looks he couldn't bear to receive.

He left, promising to return and—with emphatic casualness—Hamm Kestner, the president of the Party, declared that his position would wait for him, as (he stressed, in his very familiar tone) *you can't replace Lenz Buchmann!*

So the risings and fallings in the Buchmann house continued with a harmony that was sometimes rather like a dance; a dance *à trois*, or *à deux*, so to speak. A slow, well synchronized dance, in which on one side Lenz was getting weaker, and on the other Julia and Gustav Liegnitz were getting stronger in order to support him better; really so that these two opposing sides, united, shouldn't all collapse together.

There were two sides to this relationship, and if one of those sides weakened, the other would be left with the task of not allowing it to fall, and indeed to keep smiling, for the benefit of any spectators.

3

Harmony isn't possible, but we can try

So as the weeks passed, the Buchmann house was invaded, albeit gently, by other objects, objects *from another family*—in the sense of another human family, but also in the sense of an entirely other family of taste. The thing was, the Liegnitz siblings, in spite of all the efforts they had made, often with no support at all, still didn't have anything remotely near to the cultural consistency, the refined, noble habits and tastes of the Buchmanns, and particularly of their last living representative, Lenz Buchmann.

So the small objects that kept coming into the house brought with them another mark, the Liegnitz mark, so to speak, a mark that was the present outcome of the countless actions, events, contingencies, wills, and decisions, which over the decades the Liegnitz family had passed through, originated, resisted, etc. And so a family's artifacts, and the artifacts of their way of thinking, began to get mixed in with the objects and thoughts of Lenz Buchmann.

From a distance, and from a merely aesthetic point of view, it might be said that the Liegnitzes introduced a certain bad taste to the Buchmann house. From a lamp that Julia particularly liked and which she brought to the room where she now slept alone—a room adjacent to Lenz's so that she could be with him quickly to help with anything he asked for—to Julia and Gustav's clothes, many of which were striking in their inadequacy to the setting and their ugliness.

Gustav, now accommodated in one of the rooms on the house's lower floor, sometimes left some piece of his wardrobe on a chair, unintentionally, which soon turned into an unmistakable fact, like a number popping up in the middle of an alphabet, making any child say, "That doesn't belong there!"

Beyond the clothes and a few objects, there were also two heavy pieces of furniture transported to the Buchmann house, which had belonged to the Liegnitz family for many generations and which Julia had been unable to part with. A long wooden cupboard, about a meter high and almost four meters long, was already installed in the main room, and some of Lenz's hunting things had now been stored in it, very well organized by Julia's always solicitous hands. The other piece of Liegnitz family furniture, moved to the Buchmann house, was a table; a table that had belonged to Julia's father, Gustav Liegnitz.

Notwithstanding the strangeness of all this, it was on that table—now in one of the rooms next to the library—that Lenz was writing some notes on his political thinking, his hand getting less and less firm.

4

Of successive separate floods will the world be drowned

Another of the relevant new arrivals that cannot go unmentioned was the appearance of *Liegnitz books*, if we might call them that. That is, quite naturally, as the months went by, both Julia and Gustav started bringing some of their books into the house, ones they were reading at the time, and others that belonged to their own minuscule libraries. Among them there were some—very few, in truth—that they had inherited from the library of the Liegnitz parents. These in particular added up to no more than a dozen, but stood in brutal contrast to the carefully chosen library of the Buchmanns. They were wretched little story books, the sort consumed in their thousands by foolish adolescents and families with little culture—like the Liegnitzes.

What still sometimes irritated Buchmann—and it was now very rare that he got irritated; in fact, he really wasn't allowed to; his state of minimal organic comfort depended on his maintaining a calm equilibrium—and yet, what was still capable of troubling him profoundly was stumbling upon one of those books—*those books!*—on one of his tables or chairs.

Everything else he accepted, this was part of his characteristic survival instinct—he was well aware that his position in the world had changed and he now needed this brother and sister around him, Julia particularly. So he seemed not to notice (or pretended not to notice) how much the Liegnitz mark was coming in, bit by bit, a flow, slow but constant, into his house. And if he did notice it, he certainly didn't ascribe it too much importance.

Yet the books, yes, they did bother him. He even asked—at one point even demanded—that Julia and Gustav Liegnitz's books should remain in their respective bedrooms, and should not be left around the house.

In any case, his library, the library that joined together two strong libraries—that of Frederich Buchmann and that of Lenz Buchmann—remained inviolable, and among the most important objects and documents he kept in the drawers of his bedside table was precisely the key to that pivotal room. A library into which the Liegnitzes—out of a lack of interest (they had never asked Lenz for the key)—had never set foot.

THE EXISTENCE OF THEFT, BUT THE ABSENCE OF A THIEF

1

An alteration to sight, and to the object being observed

What had happened to Lenz Buchmann, to the proud Lenz Buchmann, that he now observed everything with such admirable placidity? Just this: Lenz Buchmann had a cancer. Or to be more precise: he had ceased to be the owner of himself; the cancer had him—the powerful Lenz had been transformed into an object.

Really, he was no longer able to think about anything, nothing was important; he quickly became nothing more than a witness— he never took his eyes off his own body, its reactions, its evolution. He made detailed analyses of whatever state he found himself in at each moment, if he felt better or worse than the previous day, if the muscles in his arms felt weaker, if his legs shook, or not, after a few minutes' standing up; all his smallest activities, then, were analyzed, by himself, from top to toe.

And more than this, gradually all his movements—however tiny or inconsequential—were observed by him in such detail that it seemed as though his illness had abruptly narrowed his field of vision at the same time as—to compensate—it had given him a great and new capacity for distinguishing minutiae. It was as though he had been endowed with a microscope that was turned exclusively on himself and that now replaced the whole variety of visual tools he once used to possess.

In times past he used to look at more things, and from more points of view; now he looked at and saw only one thing in the world—his own body—but he saw it with a new sharpness, with a depth that he had never managed before. One might have said that he had now recognized the scale of the problems involved in the simple gesture of waving good-bye to someone, and discovered too the mechanisms and countless hidden activities that a simple gesture like this implied internally. What had always seemed simple to him before, to the point of never having considered it a problem—the functioning of his body—was now, for him, the only problem.

How to get this thing to function? How to get myself out of bed with only the help of the strength in my two arms, if now my two arms have so little strength in them? What surfaces should I use to support myself?

The truth was, his illness was not a modest one. It had infiltrated the general condition of his thoughts and no longer came from the outside—this was increasingly alarming: this weakness had its origins in the intimate heritage of his body. Buchmann felt as though he were watching a thief robbing him: a distant thief who bit by bit was taking over control of what had previously been governed by the normal impulses of the species. Health gave way to action, it did not impose rules or boundaries, unlike the illness, which watched over his every movement; sometimes resembling a cautious grandmother preventing a child from running too fast, sometimes more like a sadistic gentleman who enjoys rattling off—incessantly—the list of all the activities his victim's weakness has made impossible.

THE IMPORTANCE OF NAMES

1

Wiping out what can be wiped out

Though he was very weakened by his illness, Lenz Buchmann occasionally tried to show that he was still the person managing the household, giving little orders that Julia and Gustav made as if to carry out, without discussing whether or not his instructions were reasonable. Lenz gave an order, one example being to move a piece of furniture back up from the cellar, which had been hidden away down there for some time now, because the Liegnitz siblings had long ago realized that having that piece of furniture in that particular position bothered him.

Sometimes, then, Lenz Buchmann instructed Gustav Liegnitz to carry out very particular tasks, generally manual labor, something difficult, involving some physical effort.

Symbolically, the most important of these was what Gustav was ordered to do with the bronze plaque displaying the family crest, the names of Lenz's father and mother, and also the names of himself and his brother: Albert and Lenz Buchmann.

Lenz Buchmann asked Gustav to do something that was—because of the nature of the material the plaque was made from—

extremely difficult: he asked him to eliminate one of the names—that of his brother, Albert. He should leave only the family crest, and then his father's full name—Frederich Buchmann—and then his mother's, and then his own—Lenz Buchmann. As though he had been an only child.

His mother's name was a weak name, to be sure, but its mixture with his father's blood demonstrated that there had been at least one part of her name capable of generating him. Weak, but allowing strength to remain strong—that was what Lenz thought of his mother's name.

Gustav didn't ask any questions (he didn't write them down, didn't try to speak them by making any of those long *mmm*s of his, nor did he try via any gesture). He understood exactly what the movement of Lenz's lips was articulating—lips that were now accustomed to this task, and spoke to Gustav very slowly, emphasizing every syllable.

So that there would be no doubt, with his ever more unsteady hand Lenz drew the plaque, how he wanted it to look, and marked with a clear X what he wanted Gustav to eliminate from the object.

2
An only child, at last

In the days that followed, the deaf-mute sat beside Lenz's bed—at his request—and Lenz watched the intricate manual work of scratching out each letter of his brother's name with a file. Gustav started by erasing the *A*, then the *L*.

It wasn't an impossible task by any means, but it did demand enormous patience. Principally because Lenz's desire was that it should be carried out here, in his own house, far from any eyes that might interpret or judge. It was an intimate act: a secret, family decision—so Lenz considered it, at least—which was why it hadn't gone to a workshop with much more specialized tools, which would have been able to do the job far more easily.

It was clear to Lenz Buchmann that this was not merely a job but a ceremony that had to be celebrated here, not just in his house but right beside his bed. Gustav worked on a small table and chair that he brought in to Lenz's room and then took away again after each session.

The task, thought Lenz, was being carried out by precisely the right person—the deaf-mute son of Gustav Liegnitz, the son with the same name as his father, the man Frederich Buchmann had killed. For Lenz Buchmann, the hours he spent watching the deaf-mute's slow work functioned as a sort of ritual that touched some essence inside himself he still found mysterious. Something was being done that had been left over from the previous generation. And what was that? Something he could not explain.

After the task of eliminating the name was completed, Lenz asked Gustav to give the bronze plaque a polish, so that the surviving names—especially that of his father, Frederich Buchmann, and then his own—should *shine like* (these were his exact words) *two bright lights at nighttime.*

And after three weeks, two or three hours a day, the job was done. The plaque now had only three names on it, and of these three, two that were polished with much more dedication, shining as though the letters had been inscribed the night before and not decades earlier, as was the case. The deaf-mute—so Lenz called him (his own sister sometimes asked, in a teasing tone: and the deaf-mute, where's he got to?)—the deaf-mute, Gustav, had actually done a fine job.

Between the two of them—Lenz and Gustav—and in spite of Lenz's constant mocking expression, a different relationship began to emerge, one in which Lenz increasingly came to trust the man who had until recently been merely Julia's brother, the brother to his secretary, a woman whom he already had more than enough reasons to trust entirely. He didn't look on the deaf-mute as a friend, obviously, but he did see him, at least, as someone trustworthy—an employee who did still know where the center of power was to be found.

"I've come to like your deaf-mute . . ." Lenz said to Julia one night when for the first time the bronze family plaque, raised up, slept beside him: polished, gleaming, cleansed of any impurity, and cleansed, too, at last, of the weak name of his older brother Albert, who from that moment on might never have been born.

But the following day he forgot all about this, and a few days later still, nobody could even find the plaque. There were more important matters to deal with.

WHAT METAL ARE HANDS MADE OF?

1
Forgetting a name

Amid these big transformations, big not in terms of space or dimension but in the area—if we can call it that—they took up in Lenz's consciousness, his mind, what space was now occupied by the memory of his wife? To be clear: she had always occupied an insignificant position, which insignificance had become even more apparent during the recent work undertaken by Gustav on the bronze family plaque. It hadn't been necessary to erase the name of his wife, Maria Buchmann, because that name had never been inscribed there.

The name of Lenz's wife did not appear on any object in the world that actually took up any space. On many documents, certainly—on countless pieces of paper—his wife's name was present; and around the time of her death, of her murder, in several newspapers, her name (Lenz remembered this well) had even appeared on the front page, and in the following days on the inside pages. But what was her name again?

At that moment Lenz couldn't even remember that much. What did it matter? In him—in Lenz Buchmann—not even the first letter of that name remained.

He wouldn't have been able to say that firing at Rafa the madman—whom he barely knew—and firing at his wife had been the same thing. And yet as far as he could recall, his hands, when he fired at his wife, had remained neutral, as though merely a material continuation of his weapon, and he had no recollection at any point of their having shaken.

He didn't, actually, remember any emotion at all. Neither beforehand, nor in the act itself; nor afterward, when from above—the position of a man victorious—he looked at the two bodies, trying to arrange between them the best landscape for convincing the criminal investigators of his story.

He put the two bodies in precisely the place—he remembered this—just like a theater director—and arrangement that the story in his head demanded. And at that moment, even then, what linked him to that woman wasn't sentiment but mere physical sensation—he was faced with a concrete weight that it was necessary to drag around and manipulate.

With a cynicism that he made no attempt to control, Buchmann sometimes thought that, as far as his wife was concerned—beyond the purely animal desires that she had sometimes provoked in him—the strongest impression she'd made on him was that of the weight of her dead body, a body that refused to play along and which therefore somehow seemed to encourage all her defects to rise to the surface.

He had killed his wife, and this didn't lead him to any kind of remorse. A confession or anything along those lines would have seemed an absurdity to Lenz: his sense that nothing of significance had happened was totally incompatible with getting down on his knees. Now the only recollections he retained of his wife were those that concerned her sexual activities, the way she had subjected herself—having understood certain aspects of his perversity—to the greatest humiliations, participating in the most attentive way in the games that Lenz Buchmann had devised involving other people. It was also clear to him that if his wife hadn't first discovered and then accepted and later participated in his perversions, her name would be written—in Lenz's existence—at a greater depth, and wouldn't occupy the neutral position it now had. And what was her name again? As has already been said, Buchmann already did occasionally have difficulty remembering it. But there were many other things, we should say, that he had begun to forget as well.

HIDING THE CITY'S GARBAGE

1

There are many more sounds on earth than men imagine

It has already been two weeks since Lenz Buchmann last got out of bed. A sudden downturn in the conditions of his existence had forced him, so to speak, into a retreat—he who only days earlier had gone outside, with Julia always beside him but never leaning on her, walking a few meters in the square that surrounded his house.

But his condition was now more serious, as indicated by an extreme sensitivity to noise. Both Julia and Gustav tried now not to move any household objects out of their place, and Julia—with particular care and generosity—dealt with all of Lenz's needs, her touch so light that she seemed hardly to exist, hardly to be there at all, as though able to solve problems remotely, remaining totally immobile: her presence never really noticeable, only the effects of her presence.

This new over-sensitivity to noise led Lenz Buchmann to complain to Julia about the noise that the garbage truck made when it drove past at night—around one in the morning—to collect the bags both from his house and from the other houses and buildings that were on the same square.

It should be said that nothing in the city's sanitation routine had changed. There wasn't a new truck, nor one that had suddenly started to fall apart, that for some reason was making more noise than usual; the procedures followed by the men who collected the trash were exactly the same as ever, and the time—one in the morning—had been their schedule for many years. Externally, then, there had been no change.

What had changed, and drastically so, was Lenz's body. Lenz who had always lived there and had never even noticed this work carrying on, this nighttime occurrence, this collecting of the trash.

But Lenz's new auditory sharpness and its accompanying bodily discomfort were now such that he could tell exactly which stage of the collection the garbage men had reached simply by the sounds they made. There was the jagged noise, the dreadful shrieking sound, of the garbage truck stopping, still many meters away from his house; then the vague, muffled sound that Lenz recognized as the two men—still very far from his window—jumping down from their truck (they were like some new sort of vulture, able to zero in on offal from great distances), now heading toward the trash bags that the residents had left at the doors to their buildings, then with some effort carrying them back on their shoulders, throwing them inside, into a mouth that swallowed and accepted everything.

Then—and this always came as a surprise—there were a few short seconds of silence, and how Lenz suffered in those seconds in anticipation of what was coming, or what might come. Then the truck started up again.

Another stop, a shrieking sound, closer now, the sound of the men jumping to the ground, now much clearer, sometimes a voice that startled him, almost as though a thief had just threatened him in his bedroom; a human voice in the midst of all those engine-starts, stops, and mechanical shrieks, a human voice in the middle of the garbage, getting itself right into the middle of that shapeless mass of mechanisms still functioning, of rotten food, of objects that have been amputated, undone, a human voice that shook him more than all the rest, precisely because it was human and he always feared everything that was human, always expected anything.

And then it was there, right there under his window: the noises of the machine stopping, the disgusting sound of the soft bags dropping on top of other soft bags. Sometimes the clear sound of little things coming loose from a bag that had torn, a sound that provoked a disgust in him like that he felt when faced with fatty food when his belly was already full. And again, once more, the crude comments of the men that seemed to be aimed directly at him, and then the almost sadistically slow diminishment of his suffering, with the truck moving away just a little, repeating each step, except now a few meters farther ahead; then a little farther still, farther still, until—at last—it seemed that it all had disappeared.

At these moments, Lenz always thinks it's over, but just as he's about to give a sigh of relief, there's some squeal or other—from there in the distance—or the trace of a voice, reminding him that it isn't over after all, that he'll never be quite sure, that they might, at any moment, return—either because they've forgotten to collect the trash from one house or simply because they want to torture him as much as they possibly can.

2

Why do the garbage men talk to one another?

What most annoyed him about all this was the way those men acted with complete indifference to his condition. They surely knew that this was Lenz Buchmann's house, and they surely knew—everybody knew now—that he was ill, that he had a serious illness, which was why this casualness, those constant repeated voices, were inconceivable; the voices on top of everything else, demonstrating their utter disregard to his suffering. Why did they not—at the very least—do their work in silence? Why did they need to talk? What did they have to say to one another? What did a man who carried a bag that emitted an absolutely inhuman stench—or an all-too-human one, rather, or the stench that remains when a human has finished satisfying himself—what could such a man, then, have to say to another such man, another man carrying garbage? What could they talk about? Did they tell jokes? Did they comment on some article in the paper? Talk about their children? Why did they have to talk at all? Why not staff this job with deaf-mutes? Gustav, poor old Gustav Liegnitz, would be perfect. Why would someone who carried trash need to speak and hear? All they have to do is use their eyes—locate the black bags at the entrances to buildings and then simply carry them from one place to another—making them disappear from people's normal lives and expelling them who-knows-where, though in any event to a place characterized by being remote: we wouldn't be able to bear the smell that a single week of our lives would leave behind! How good, yes, to take it all far away; put the garbage somewhere far away, but do it in silence!

Buchmann decided to complain to Julia. He said that she should go talk to his colleague Hamm Kestner—the president of the Party. He would surely understand. Have the garbage men change their procedures, collect the trash from that square in the late morning—an excellent time for it. It would be easy to resolve the matter, said Buchmann, it was just a matter of scheduling that one activity in the late morning, he insisted. At that time—said Buchmann—I'm never asleep. Noise matters little to me at that time. They can talk all they want. If they want—if they have any reason to—they can even sing, said Lenz Buchmann.

3

President Kestner continues to be understanding

When Julia came home that evening her face at first glance revealed nothing—nothing positive or negative. She then explained to Dr. Buchmann that she had spoken directly to Kestner, which was an absolutely exceptional event and worth mentioning: besides, Kestner had sent Lenz a big hug—*a brotherly hug*—those were his very words, Kestner repeated them and then asked me to repeat them back to him; he wished you a speedy recovery, he said that soon he'd be coming to visit you, that he's just waiting for a crucial question to be resolved; he also said that your office—the vice president's office—is untouched, being kept for you, and that even Mr. Buchmann has forgotten about a book he was always reading and that he left in the building and the president didn't even give it back to me because he says the book is there waiting for you, waiting for your return at full strength, he said that they need your strong arm and ideas. And he also said that yesterday the ceremony commemorating the first anniversary of the theater attack went exceptionally well, and that your name—as the greatest brain in the city, in Kestner's words—I'm just repeating what he said, said Julia—that your name was mentioned by various people who were giving speeches and that he himself repeated your name three times—three times, he emphasized that—Mr. Lenz Buchmann. He told me, too, that it's not possible to alter the procedures or the schedules of the garbage collection, which have been set for years and which work effectively; he told me, too, that given how important the city is to you, he was sure, he said, that you'd understand; that in any case he would give orders for the trash-collectors to moderate their conversations; he promised that the trash would be collected in the most complete silence, as though—these were his words—the men weren't carrying detritus but sitting at a wake, in utter silence; he told me, too, that he's sure that Mr. Lenz Buchmann would soon be sleeping well again; and he also reminded me that he's still got—he'll give it to you later in person—a plaque that was donated in your name—*to Dr. Lenz Buchmann with Friendship*—by the Association of Ancient Fighters, to which your father belonged, and that that Association is soon going to be arranging a tribute to Mr. Buchmann, a simple tribute, but one that demonstrates all the friendship the city has for you; finally, when I was on my way out, President Kestner insisted that next week at the latest he would be coming to visit, and then he wants you on your feet to receive him with a hug more vigorous than a twenty year old's; and then, he also said . . .

It was here that Lenz Buchmann made a firm gesture for Julia to be quiet. And Julia was quiet.

A NIGHTTIME TASK

1

Let the bells toll at the movement of my hand

The unusual request that Lenz Buchmann, toward the end of his life, made of Gustav Liegnitz was accepted by Gustav—no doubt—as irrational, a totally absurd desire, but one which, because it came from a body now wasting away a little more each day, could not be refused.

Lenz asked Gustav to spread a certain phrase around the city. That, during the night, hidden from everyone else, he should write it on the walls between properties, on the walls of houses, on the outside walls of public buildings—in short, everywhere.

And he asked him, too, for complete secrecy. That he mention it to no one. Not even to his sister, Julia. And Lenz even recommended Gustav a particular kind of durable paint that it was almost impossible to scrape off or erase, which meant that if anyone wanted the phrase to disappear they would have to get the wall repainted. Then, on a piece of paper, he wrote down the name of the paint brand in question, and also wrote—in tiny letters—the phrase that Gustav Liegnitz was to scatter across the whole city over a single night.

That was an important detail: it had to be done in a single night, to avoid any subsequent obstacles. It was a crime to paint on walls, whether private or public. Writing Lenz's phrase on some buildings would in fact be extremely dangerous for Gustav, as certain properties would probably have security.

Lenz was extremely thorough: he went on to write down all the sites, all the walls on which the phrase should appear. And he made his request in the form of a demand that could not under any circumstances be denied.

Two nights later, Gustav Liegnitz, the mute Gustav Liegnitz, carried out—on his own—an act that, from a purely practical point of view, was quite admirable, and which was only made possible thanks to enormous physical effort and unusual skill.

The next day, the first light of morning revealed a new city to the earliest risers.

Scattered across countless walls—many of them on the plan proposed by Lenz and some that weren't, but nonetheless all standing out like garish stains, even around the back of the main Party building—there was that phrase flooding and invading the city and so forcing its citizens to stop, astonished.

Written in black on the red-brick wall of a primary school, the phrase: *Death to Lenz Buchmann!*

A few meters ahead, on the front façade of the post office: *Death to Lenz Buchmann!*

Right alongside that, on a residential building, along one of its sides: *Death to Lenz Buchmann!*

On a narrow street that opened into one of the city's main squares, on a wall: *Death to Lenz Buchmann!*

On the pavement in the lower part of the city: *Death to Lenz Buchmann!*

In a corner, half-hidden, of one of the walls of the central hospital: *Death to Lenz Buchmann!*

On the wall of a well-known law firm: *Death to Lenz Buchmann!*

On the outside wall of a kindergarten: *Death to Lenz Buchmann!*

On the license plate of a bus: *Death to Lenz Buchmann!*

At the entrance to one of the city's public gardens, right on the ground: *Death to Lenz Buchmann!*

On the white external wall of a public lavatory in the same park: *Death to Lenz Buchmann!*

On a monument to the dead of the last war, beginning at the base of the statue and finishing halfway up: *Death to Lenz Buchmann!*

On the trunk of a tree—probably one of Gustav's improvisations, since such elements weren't on the list—from bottom to top: *Death to Lenz Buchmann!*

On a maternity hospital, on various private buildings, on two cars that were parked on one of the roads that opened into the main square, in the main square itself, on the marble base that surrounded the fountain and also on the front façade of the bank located in this same square, on the main façade of two smaller headquarters of the Party, as well as the back—already mentioned—of the main headquarters, and also on the building where retired soldiers used to go to collect their pensions, on the back part of one of the city's libraries, and, finally, on the main façade of the Buchmann family house itself, the phrase, painted in black: *Death to Lenz Buchmann! Death to Lenz Buchmann! Death to Lenz Buchmann!*

CONSULTING THE TIMETABLE

1
Losing control, or creating a world?

Sitting on his bed, in his sleepwear and with his hands trembling—as though traveling by way of the vehicle now concerning him, suspended in its rocking movements—Lenz Buchmann had for several long minutes been trying, without success, to consult the train timetable, and from this consultation to draw some conclusions. The tremor in his hands—more pronounced every day—was so intense at that moment that Buchmann couldn't really match up a line and column, or not with any certainty: the departure and arrival times that, on this timetable, were arranged vertically, seemed to be flying away—or at least taking a detour—from the names of the cities, the locations of the stops, which occupied the horizontal lines.

The following day marked the twentieth anniversary of his father's death, and Lenz, overcoming objections from Julia and the doctor who was taking care of him, expressed a desire to travel to the city of Frederich Buchmann's birth, which was also where he had been buried. It was a significant date.

Julia had already offered to choose the departure and arrival times, but Lenz insisted; he wanted to be the one to decide.

The situation, then, was darkly ridiculous. In Lenz's hands the little timetable trembled: the times and the cities swayed, seemingly shifting position at every moment, and he couldn't manage to make them stand still, couldn't concentrate on the simple crossing of a line with a column.

Julia was there beside him, however, looking at the little railway leaflet, trying—without Lenz noticing it—to steady his hand slightly, holding it as though in a gentle caress. And with her free hand, Julia was also trying to point at the line that indicated with a clear—and vast—name the point in the world where they currently were, and then run her finger slowly down that line, thereby showing Lenz the possible departure times.

"8:45, 9:30, 10:15, 11:00, 11:45 . . ."—and she stopped there. Later would be of no interest. "You want to go in the morning, don't you Mr. Buchmann? It's better . . ."

Lenz Buchmann nodded yes; that they would leave in the morning.

Julia went on, gently:

"The journey takes two hours. If we leave at 11:45 we'd arrive close to two o'clock. That seems rather late to me, don't you think?"

It was late, Lenz agreed. The 8:45 and 9:30 departures were, on the other hand, too early.

"10:15? We'll arrive a little after twelve."

Lenz asked Julia to show him that particular train again on the timetable, and so Julia again ran the index finger of her left hand along the horizontal line, showing the time of departure; and then, bringing the same finger down a little, she ran along the horizontal line that showed the arrivals. She stopped at the arrival time in question—12:10—and then moved back up the small distance she'd moved down, but now within the same column, indicating—again—the departure. And she said again, as though speaking to a child:

"The train leaves here at 10:15 and arrives there at 12:10. It's perfect."

Lenz agreed.

In his hands, however, the timetable wouldn't stop shaking.

At that moment, exhausted by the effort of self-restraint that making this one small decision had demanded of her, it occurred to Julia—when she saw how Lenz's hands shook—that Mr. Buchmann looked as though he was shuffling cards, moving some back and others forward; or, more precisely, shuffling cities and times, switching around the order of the cities and their locations as well as their temporal order.

Dissociated from the fact that such movements were the result of a serious illness, Lenz's gestures conveyed a sense of power, or at least of an illusion of power, that was utterly divine: if in the past someone had observed this same man (Lenz Buchmann) and this same situation (hands shaking while holding a train timetable) they might have believed that the man (Lenz Buchmann) considered himself capable—with just this movement of his hands—of shuffling, disordering, destroying—in sum—the established order of the world; affecting the proper position of each person in space as well as within their accustomed chronological structures.

At another time—and we're speaking not of centuries now but a single year's difference—back in the days when Lenz Buchmann himself occupied a different position, this trembling of his hands wouldn't have been taken for tremors provoked by some illness, but seen as a divine trembling, the trembling of someone who, re-positioning cities and times, elevating them to a new plane—and with them, men, and all of nature as well—really was creating a new world.

AT THE TRAIN STATION

1

Ascertaining that we do not receive looks from other people in the same way that they give them

It had been many years since Lenz had traveled by train. He had chosen this mode of transport in part because it linked him to happy memories of his childhood. Apart from that, he wanted this journey—which would probably be his last visit to his father's gravestone—to be as discreet as possible, and Lenz felt at this point (unsupported by any logical rationale) that the best way to accomplish this would be traveling surrounded by a mass of anonymous people.

He and Julia arrived too early, however—the cautious earliness that Julia now built into any of their movements—which left them exposed in the train station in a way Lenz certainly hadn't wanted. Their train left at 10:15, and it was still only 9:10 when, their tickets already in hand, Julia and Mr. Buchmann sat down on one of the benches inside the station to wait.

The busyness there was at its usual level—and, indeed, at that time of the morning, particularly intense. Some of the people who passed them—just arrived, or heading for the departure platforms—couldn't take their eyes off the strange couple: a young woman and a thin, very thin man; so thin, in fact, and with such an expression, it was clear to everyone that he was seriously ill. No doubt the people who passed them saw a daughter with her father. The dedicated daughter who accompanies her sick father everywhere.

Noticing these glances, Lenz Buchmann understood them to be—without exception—looks of recognition: here was the powerful Dr. Lenz Buchmann, still vice president of the Party. But it was not so.

Few people—perhaps just one or two—could have identified that cadaverous, ravaged man as the vice president of the Party. It should be added, however, that many of the people who didn't recognize him wouldn't have recognized him even if he had retained his former healthy appearance from photographs and other well-known images.

What interest did these people have in politics? Did they ever look at any faces too closely, apart from those of their immediate family—children, wife, husband—and perhaps of a few dangerous neighbors? Even when Lenz was healthy, fleshier, with good color, his face wouldn't have meant anything to them. They had no idea that this face, a month earlier, had been on the verge of positioning itself directly above (just a few centimeters above) a right hand (a hand, that is, belonging to the same body) that could, under the right circumstances, sign laws that would utterly change their lives and the conditions of their existence—these people who now, in a hurry, had no idea of the significance of this man or of his decline, never stopping their forward motion, fixated on getting out of the station as quickly as possible—to another city or to some precisely located shelter, a place more comfortable than the station.

They were like herbivores who, despite so many centuries of training, still had no idea how to identify carnivores—not even the one animal that, thanks to its proximity and speed, was their primary predator.

So these people passed, distracted, from one side of the station to the other, seeing a sick man as a sick man, but completely incapable of seeing in that now sick man someone who, months earlier, had been the most dangerous animal of all, one that had threatened every one of them; who had been ready for anything and to whom other people—like these now passing—were the trash of humanity, the remains that other, more decisive men had left behind, so that—if possible—if necessary—the city's sanitation services could collect them and take them far away, to somewhere else, whence their stench could not possibly return.

The wolf was sick, and no one even recognized him as one.

2

*From the boarding platform to the seat in the carriage; or two
times that do not always coincide*

Like well-behaved little boys, at ten o'clock Julia and Buchmann
were already outside on the boarding platform, looking nervously
at the still empty space where the people would soon line up, a
space that seemed to be announcing the arrival of something
quite grand, not merely the arrival of a train.

Ten minutes before the set time, Lenz Buchmann was already
complaining that the train wasn't running according to schedule,
and a moment later was accusing Julia of not having consulted the
timetable correctly.

From time to time, in what might have appeared to be no more
than a tic, Buchmann stroked a little piece of metal—a key, in
his pocket—with his left hand. Hidden from prying eyes, his left
hand—or, to be more precise, the fingers of his left hand—carried
out the same sort of movements as a believer would with a cross
or a rosary in his pocket—or else a compass to be consulted with
one's fingers at exact intervals.

Bit by bit the boarding platform began to fill up.

A mother with a child, with a firm, powerful right hand that wouldn't let her child run off, as it seemed to want to; a whole family, two children, aged perhaps nine and ten, their parents calm, all under control; and more men and then vulgar couples, some of them obviously yokels with the look of people ready to flee from the big city to take shelter back on their little parcels of land, back down their mole-holes. A lot of people, the jostle of suitcases, a few shouts, assorted disjointed conversations, and then, after a given moment, a collective, synchronized anxiety: it was ten-thirteen and the train should be about to arrive; necks were craned forwards and to the side, feet left down where they were, and dozens of eyes turned to face in the same direction: a spatial direction—the train was coming from there, from that side—but a temporal one too. They were there, it seemed to them, with their eyes turned toward ten-fifteen, and that specific time seemed about to appear, in material form, there, along those rails.

Sometimes one of the pairs of eyes swung between the great station clock (confirming the precise time) and the still empty tracks, like someone with two clocks trying to set one by the other. But in reality there weren't two clocks. At most there were two times: one, the planned, predicted one, the other, the actual time—meant to gain substance there in the train—the time in which things really happened, a visible time that didn't obey any mechanism controlled by man; and this was especially evident just then as the station clock was showing 10:23 and there was still no train.

They were standing at one machine—the clock—which signaled the arrival of another—the train. And still the two machines weren't working right, they were out of sync: what men desired and what they had set down on paper did not coincide. How, then, to get times right, taking account of all the other occurrences that the world and men produce? That's the difficulty, thought the weakened Lenz, they so rarely meet—two things that one wants to see occur, actually happening together in the desired time and space.

But at last the train arrived, and the crowd advanced upon it with an abruptness that only in a few cases caused the speed of boarding the carriage to overwhelm the last vestiges of their good manners.

In this regard, Lenz Buchmann was the target of a gentleness that few people on that boarding platform (perhaps some other old man, a child, or a mother with a baby in her arms) could have enjoyed: they let him go on ahead.

So Lenz got into the carriage while, behind him, Julia helped him with a little push that she tried to transmit as discreetly as possible.

Then—inside now—they found their seats and sat down, side by side. Lenz Buchmann with the tiredness and the satisfaction of someone who after a long ascent has arrived at the top of a mountain.

"Are you tired, Mr. Buchmann?"

Mr. Buchmann couldn't even reply; he just raised his fragile right hand in a clear signal to Julia to wait. He would speak when he had recovered his usual rate of respiration.

Many kilometers later, Mr. Buchmann replied that, yes, he was tired.

THE RETURN TO HIS FATHER'S TOMB

1

A conversation with no witnesses. What was said? Who spoke?

And here they are now, on their way back, Julia and Mr. Buchmann; many kilometers are behind them, now, between them and the city of Frederich Buchmann's birth, and more specifically, the only point in the little city that Lenz was interested in: his father's tomb.

Those moments, beside Frederich Buchmann's tomb, had been of an intensity that could not be understood or shared by anyone else. Julia, with her remarkable discretion, seemed to have disappeared.

A few meters from the tomb she had slowed her pace and let go of Lenz's arm, which she had previously been holding, and as she allowed Buchmann to make his way forward on his own, with his slow, struggling steps, she herself stopped, took a few steps off to one side, and turned away, almost as if—though never taking her eyes off of Mr. Buchmann, as it seemed he might fall over at any moment—she was looking somewhere else. And her discretion and correctness were such that, in those intimate moments, she even made herself think about something else, mentally moving herself away from her present location, and transmitting—at least to herself—the impression that she was giving the dying Lenz Buchmann more room to say good-bye to his father. Because—even though one was still alive and the other already dead—what was really taking place was a good-bye between two men.

The fact that Lenz was dying—already so obvious—made it a particularly strange reunion, a rather unusual leave-taking: *the one who is dying is saying good-bye to the one already dead.* What could Julia do in the middle of such a good-bye? Pretty Julia, though always discreet, Julia so full of life and strength, what could she do there, standing between the dying man and this man who seemed not to have been alive for some time?

She felt as though, if those two men could have spoken to one another, she wouldn't have understood a single word. Even if they were all speaking the same language, she, Julia, like a fool, a cretin, thought she wouldn't be able to understand the meaning of a single phrase.

During this time, while something completely alien to her was happening between the two men—between father and son—Julia thought about herself, only now about herself. And she thought, at this precise moment, about how urgent it was becoming that she find herself a husband, and, above all, how urgent it was becoming for her not to *find* (an act that seems little related to one's individual energy and will) but to *make* (a much firmer word, that)—how urgent it was for her to make a child.

There are certain thoughts that—however much one might try to convince oneself that they oughtn't to be entertained, owing perhaps to some moral law—one can't in reality help playing host to. This was what was happening to Julia in those moments alone, when she made herself think of something other than the balance or lack of balance in Mr. Buchmann's two supporting limbs.

And then Julia did think about her boss, about the man who—via an almost accidental encounter—had changed her life, and she felt (though she tried hard not to) that she was becoming distanced from his state of decline. At that moment, what she needed was a young man, a strong man, who would make her move forward. What surrounded her now was no longer her world. She was young.

Julia quickly abandoned these thoughts, so inappropriate to that setting. But now Mr. Buchmann is coming back—from where? that's the question; and from what? that's a question to be asked too. He's returning, then—and someone watching these events might reply, simply enough: (from where?) a tomb, and (from what?) from a conversation. Our only remaining uncertainty: whether, in this conversation, Lenz spoke, or only listened.

2

Little movements lost on a little journey

Julia is someone whose careful attentiveness never ceases. She protects Lenz in all situations, at every moment. She anticipates the train's every little jerk, leaning in such a way that her weight supports Buchmann's; as the train brakes, she puts her arm out—like a mother for her child—so that Buchmann doesn't tip over; she straightens up his head, very gently, whenever he falls asleep, trying to find the best position for him. Julia, in short, is the very model of a strong woman who is always taking care, anticipating dangers, and, if necessary, facing down enemies—even if these should be on an almost laughable scale.

A young man who, as he makes his way down the aisle, almost falls, thanks to the swaying of the train, and this on Mr. Buchmann, who in the meantime has fallen asleep again—that is an enemy to be faced down. A woman of broad physique, who—boarding at some station or other—sits in the seat opposite Buchmann, occupying (owing to the nature of her bulk) a great deal of space, far more than her assigned lot—she is another enemy to be faced down by Julia, while Mr. Buchmann sleeps, stripped completely of any instincts toward self-defense: his mouth ostentatiously open and with a little thread of saliva hanging in the corner, a thread that is consistently renewed, despite Julia's regular wiping.

At last the two of them arrive at their starting-point, at the station, Julia feeling that they've arrived "safe and sound," and Mr. Buchmann too showing a change of mood, a kind of joy, so to speak, as though he had both fulfilled a duty and extinguished some fear that Julia could not understand.

It is worth noting that during this return, and later, at the station, and in all the moments that followed, Mr. Buchmann didn't once repeat that tic of his, his left hand in his pocket stroking, turning, moving the key from one side to another; and this was because he hadn't come back with the key that he had taken to the city of his father Frederich's birth.

AN UNFORESEEN INTIMACY

1

Julia

Dr. Lenz Buchmann was lying down, his eyes open, and Julia, sitting beside him on the bed, was stroking his face, as she so often does.

On that day, however, something different happened. There was something in Buchmann's body that responded; he was excited.

Julia noticed, and quite naturally her hand began to move down Mr. Buchmann's face to his chest, first, and then to his penis.

She touched it, lightly, almost accidentally, but then her hand moved back and her fingers wrapped around its base. She began, slowly, to move her fingers up and move them down, up and down, always slowly, as though she weren't there and her fingers weren't doing what they were doing.

Julia Liegnitz went on; it was the first time that this had happened; she didn't know whether she was really meant to keep going, or whether, on the contrary, she ought to stop. She didn't even dare look at Mr. Buchmann's face, she didn't want to. She only knew that he wasn't saying a word, he was completely silent, which she took to mean that she should continue, and she continued, moving her hand up and down, always the same rhythm, as though she had all the time in the world—there was no hurry at all.

Then she dared to look at Buchmann out of the corner of her eye. He had his eyes closed, which for a moment scared Julia. The idea went through her head that Dr. Buchmann had died there, at that moment—but no. He had closed his eyes, but he was awake and clearly breathing. She turned her eyes away from that face and continued to move her hand up and down along the penis of Dr. Lenz Buchmann, vice president of the Party, formally speaking, and still the second most important man in the city; son of the late Frederich Buchmann, renowned soldier who had given a new impetus to the fortunes of his family, a family that with this son had attained the highest reputation that any family could aspire to.

And this was the moment that—all of a sudden—a tiny gray mouse ran from one side of the room to the other.

Julia was startled, she instinctively stopped the movement of her hand on Buchmann's penis and got up from the bed, trying to see where the mouse had gone. Where had the creature come from?

On her feet already, Julia looked into the corners of the room—she could no longer see the mouse—where did it get to?

Lenz Buchmann, meanwhile, had opened his eyes. He did nothing else, perhaps he had no more strength, all that's certain is that he made no movement nor was there any noticeable change in his expression.

Julia looked around her, caught between the shock of seeing the mouse and her desire to forget she'd seen it; soon she sat back down on to the bed. A few seconds of confusion, trying to work out where she was, what was going on; then her hand returned to

Buchmann's penis, first with excessive haste, and then, after a few moments, returning to the same slow rhythm of movement, up and down.

Buchmann, meanwhile, closed his eyes again.

SIGNIFICANT CHANGES TO THE HOUSEHOLD

1

The world doesn't stop

It's already been two weeks since Lenz Buchmann stopped having any control whatsoever over more than the square meter immediately surrounding him—and even this vigilance was only visual. He could no longer get up—the weakness of his arms and legs wouldn't allow it—and this condition led to the deaf-mute Gustav, at his sister's suggestion, taking a television set to the sick man's bedroom; this was a piece of equipment that Lenz Buchmann had always ignored, as it encouraged a passivity that he was naturally unable to tolerate; but it was left nonetheless on top of the piece of furniture immediately opposite the bed; a television set which in the days that followed remained permanently switched on.

This even more alarming turn in Buchmann's condition, as well as the formalizing of his will, which put the Liegnitzes—this was how Gustav thought of it, although the property was in Julia's name only—formally and legally in a different position . . . these two factors combined were what faced the two Liegnitz siblings with a set of new administrative tasks on an enormous scale.

All told, the deaf-mute—as Gustav continued to be addressed by Buchmann—perfected his decision-making skills very quickly. In just a few weeks, he had made a number of important decisions—he, all by himself, with the encouragement (given with a certain apathy and indifference) of Julia, most of whose energies were still focused on caring for Lenz: from the dismissing of a worker whom Gustav really didn't like, to the sale of a small plot of land; an insignificant plot, but its sale allowed the household (while other, larger questions remained as yet unresolved) to have the means to deal with a set of urgent financial necessities.

Likewise, if some former frequenter of the Buchmann house had chosen this moment to revisit the space, he would no doubt have experienced quite a shock, pinched himself several times, and gone back out through the front door to make sure he hadn't got the wrong building. The interior had undergone some rather profound changes. From the furniture it contained, to the objects that were kept there—in terms of their locations, but also in terms of actual material content—everything, in short, that dated from *the old house*, if we can call it that, was now someplace different, or had disappeared to parts unknown.

At the same time, like a very slow—but constant—flood, day after day saw the arrival of new objects, papers, and files belonging to the deaf-mute and Julia, and also, now, with no self-restraint, several objects, photos, and another two heavy pieces of furniture inherited from the Liegnitz family. Given that the contents of the *old house* had not—obviously—evaporated into thin air, what was now objectively Julia Liegnitz's house displayed an almost grotesque mixture of elements, materials, and tastes—a mixture, ultimately, of materials and tastes coming from two families with completely different traditions, habits, and histories.

The *new house*, however, as we said above, was still in flux. Things were progressing.

PROGRESSING TO THE END

1

The lock

On one particular morning, a few minutes after Julia had left the house to deal with some urgent matters, leaving Mr. Buchmann asleep, comfortably, Gustav Liegnitz, the deaf-mute, decided that he was not going to let this day pass without taking action. He had thought about it several times before and he had already made his decision. That was why, on this day, he didn't even need a moment to get himself ready. He knew his sister would be against it, so this was the moment.

He went up, then, to the next floor, having looked in on Lenz's room, where he was fast asleep, and there, on the upper floor, standing at the closed library door, he made a first sharp movement with his right hand, pushing and pulling the door handle.

No one knew anything about the key to the library. What had happened? Where was the key? Buchmann couldn't remember where he'd put it, and Julia, with a complete lack of interest in the contents of the Buchmann library, hadn't bothered to pursue the question. And so the room had just stayed, just sat, for months, the door closed; it was the only room in the house the Liegnitzes had never been inside.

The deaf-mute tried, then—with little jerks and jolts, forward and back, left and right—to work the lock loose. It was obvious, however, that he would need something more.

The deaf-mute, this younger Liegnitz, then moved a short distance away from the library door and stopped for a few seconds. And he chose that moment, all at once—when perhaps you might have thought he was about to go around the house looking for tools to help him open the door—and perhaps surprising even himself—he threw himself sideways, pitching all the weight of his body against the library door. The crashing sound heard at that moment barely had time to play itself out completely—that is, to diminish gradually in volume till it had disappeared—because there was another crash immediately following, and then another and another: four, five, six, seven, eight, nine times, the whole weight of Gustav's body against that lock. And he heard it like someone underwater in a swimming pool hears the shouts of someone above, in the air. What he was doing seemed—due to his physical deficiency—to be happening at a great distance.

The task, however, had set itself definitively in Gustav the deaf-mute's head, and now no retreat was possible. There was a job to do—to break down that door—and he wasn't going to leave till he had completed it.

Then he gave a kick, facing forward at first. And then, because it seemed to him that he might be able to use more force the other way, he turned his back on the door and gave a kick backward, a back-kick, if that's the word, another back-kick, and yet another, and now this human form seemed capable only of movements that—if seen by an outside observer—would have to be classified as bestial.

Giving himself a few meters' space, he then advanced, like a bull. As fast as he could, and now always from the side, so as not to hurt himself, he charged against the door, taking on the nature at that moment not of a creature but of a compact mass designed to knock things down. He concentrated himself completely—limbs in, shoulders likewise curled inward—and advanced at full speed against the door, provoking an impressive series of crashing sounds.

At a certain point during all this, it occurred to him that the noise—which entered him like a tiny, distant thud, but which in the outside world was of a quite different intensity—might already have woken Mr. Buchmann. He immediately overwhelmed this thought, however, with a silent exclamation—*what do I care!*—as well as with the immediate understanding that even if Buchmann did hear something, he wouldn't be able to make it up the stairs. And this sense of another man's weakness gave Gustav renewed strength; and forgetting the intense pain he was already feeling on one side of his body and in both his arms, Gustav Liegnitz, the deaf-mute, undertaking a bit of manual labor, involving great physical effort, which for him took place in almost complete silence—which calmed him, in a sense, or at least stopped him getting annoyed—gathered his last ounce of strength, took himself a good four meters away from the already partly-broken door, launched himself at it, and *bang!*, a crashing noise, the lock broke, the door opened, and with absolutely no possibility of stopping himself, Gustav Liegnitz found himself hurled, a heavy bullet, against the floor of the Buchmann library.

Still on the floor, he looked around him, and saw there really were only books. But he was happy, very happy.

COMPASSION IS FOREVER

1
Not charity

From time to time the tramp, whose name Lenz had never known, knocked at the door to ask for food and charity. It was always Julia who answered, and understanding that the tramp had been, and still was—for Lenz had not died yet—protected within that house, Julia always offered him a full meal, which she would carefully wrap up and hand to him. She had no idea about the countless episodes of intimacy that this tramp had witnessed in that same house, almost always in the kitchen, with Dr. Lenz Buchmann and his late wife. And the tramp, this tramp, whose ever-alert survival instinct had understood at once that things had changed, changed completely around there, maintained the most astonishing discretion on the subject of his relationship with that powerful man.

Sometimes he asked after the health of the owner of the house: "Dr. Buchmann, how is he?"

Julia would reply vaguely, sometimes with a dishonest *He's better* or *He's getting better*, and the tramp would say that that was just as well, please send the doctor his respectful greetings, that he was grateful for all his kindness and the girl's, and that he was sure that next time he came to the house it would be Dr. Lenz himself, fully restored to health, who would receive him.

The days went on, of course, and all conditions changed—those of the healthy as much as those of the sick—as is the way with human nature when you mix it up with time; and the occasional hostile reaction from Gustav, or even from Julia—along with the gradual reduction in the quality and the quantity of the alms given—meant that, slowly and surely, the tramp stopped coming back to the Buchmann house with the same frequency. Until, at last, to the relief of the Liegnitzes, he stopped being seen in the area altogether.

NOT FORGETTING WHAT MUST NOT BE FORGOTTEN

1

Learning to read

Lenz's memory, as has already been said, was weakening to a degree that would shock any former acquaintances who saw him now.

Over the course of the gradual evolution of his illness, and especially from the moment when it became apparent throughout the city that Lenz was not simply ill but dying, the number of his visitors began to increase, and their visits came with increasing frequency. Old colleagues from the hospital, former Party colleagues, distant relatives—in short, countless people approached his bed (and then, naturally, moved away again). Only President Kestner, due to a series of official obligations, was unable to visit Lenz at this time.

And it wasn't without a certain amount of shock that these visitors first encountered what was left of Lenz's body; a body that seemed to be disappearing into itself, sucked away by some degenerative mechanism that was apparently the only thing left in him that still worked. But the shock of seeing Lenz's state of physical degeneration was followed by a second shock, which in every visitor went on to shake up a whole series of their convictions about human existence, free will, the capacity for choice. This second shock was the result of the confirmation that Lenz no longer remembered any one of them. (Julia would say, making an effort to remind him—Mr. Buchmann, this is the doctor who operated on you, remember?)

Do you remember?

Buchmann did not remember.

He didn't remember the names, the circumstances in which he had met these people, the familiarity he used to have with this or that face, the events they might have witnessed together, etc. etc. And, in fact, the most shocking detail about this already shocking state of affairs was the formality that Lenz maintained toward those with whom he had once been close: *And you, sir—where do I know you from?*

It sometimes seemed as though his weakness hadn't suspended the instinct for safety that had always forced him away from other people, kept them at a distance. Then he'd kept them away with arguments, with looks or decisions, but now—completely exposed and fragile—he defended himself, perhaps intuitively, certainly with no awareness that he was doing it, with that *sir*, with that formal mode of address.

His memory was in serious condition. And the degeneration was advancing at great speed. An almost incomprehensible speed. It hadn't yet happened with Julia, but a few days earlier Lenz Buchmann had failed to recognize Gustav Liegnitz. Doesn't that one ever talk? he asked Julia. And she explained to him that this man was her brother, that he had lived there in that house for several months: he was Gustav Liegnitz—and Lenz repeated the name, intensely—who was responsible for looking after the place.

Sometimes, however, his memory seemed to return, all of a sudden, in a rush of clear-sightedness that soon afterward—minutes or hours afterward—would disappear.

With only the slightest awareness of what was happening to him, an awareness that, somewhere else, in the depths of his cadaverous body, he was trying to resist, Lenz awoke one morning with the feeling—which he then confirmed—that he couldn't remember his father's name.

That same day he asked Julia to write down his father's full name on a piece of paper and to put the piece of paper on his bedside table.

Frederich? he asked, the first time he read the name. Julia replied yes:

"Frederich Taubert Buchmann, your father's full name."

"Frederich?" asked Lenz.

"Yes," Julia assured him, "that was your father's first name."

In the days that followed, at nighttime, Lenz Buchmann, with an almost imperceptible movement, would ask for the piece of paper, and Julia would put it in his hands. Then—it resembled a childhood reading exercise—Lenz would murmur the name that was written there, his father's name, repeating it several time before—tired—asking Julia to put the piece of paper away carefully. Then, he would fall asleep.

THE CENTER SHIFTS

1

Even the deaf-mute wants to take part

In the final phase of Dr. Buchmann's illness, his relationship to the deaf-mute Gustav altered dramatically.

Gustav Liegnitz had put up with a lot in his life. He had been teased since childhood. He was then able to breathe a little easier for a bit, later, when he found himself surrounded by adults who at least controlled their sarcasm and the sense of superiority they felt when they were around him. In spite of this, there had never been a time when he'd been able to rest.

He understood that whatever happened around him, or whatever happened to him, whether he became rich or not, whether he earned some prestige or not, whether or not he made progress professionally, whether or not he had a beautiful woman at his side, he would always be a deaf-mute, someone for whom all sounds were distant—other people only existed for him through their movements—and who could only try to communicate through drawn-out *mmm*s. This feeling of being harassed, that he would never be able to free himself, had recently returned, more profoundly than ever, due to his closeness to Dr. Lenz Buchmann. What that man had done to transform his life so radically—what Gustav had to look forward to now was quite different to what he could ever have dreamed of in the past—this almost magical change had always felt somewhat deflated by the superiority and sarcasm with which Lenz Buchmann always addressed him, in the days when Buchmann was healthy and strong; and then, strange though this may seem, even more intensely following his illness. Gustav couldn't actually remember a single time, before he'd fallen ill, that Lenz had referred to him as *the deaf-mute*, and not by his name. Whereas, after the illness had presented itself, and as it worsened, Buchmann had begun to address him constantly as *deaf-mute*; just like that, as though that were his name. And he used the term in his absence—Where's the deaf-mute?—as much as in his presence—So, deaf-mute, you've arrived, then?

Which was why it should be no surprise that as Lenz Buchmann lost his capacities—first physical, then mental—something had also been changing in Gustav Liegnitz's body, his movements, indeed, his whole mental structure. It wasn't that he was thinking of revenge, or anything of the sort. Far from it: a part of him was deeply thankful—and couldn't be otherwise—for the way Dr. Buchmann had transformed his sister's life and his own. It wasn't a matter of revenge, then, or of any such other action on a large scale, but a feeling that, each day, the right to use such comprehensive sarcasm was moving from Lenz's hands into his own. And he— Gustav Liegnitz—was a man; he did not waste such opportunities.

So little episodes arose, sarcasm coming now from a new point of origin—the center was shifting.

They were small episodes, insignificant. Gustav—he could feel it—now had the right, because he had the strength, to make fun of Dr. Buchmann (albeit with some restraint), without his noticing it. But it never got out of hand. Apart from one time.

2

Games that you can play with someone who has lost his reason

Let us talk about that one time.

For the first time that past year, Julia had to be away from the old Buchmann house for two days—the house that, though no one in the city would call it this, was now the Liegnitz house. As she was the only legitimate manager of Lenz Buchmann's estate, she was the only person who could hope to make some progress on a number of bureaucratic procedures relating to certain old pieces of property that were still in Lenz's father's name. So she found herself having to return to the city of Frederich Buchmann's birth, this time without Lenz's company.

When she found herself alone on the train, with no need to channel all her vigilance and attention toward another body, Julia felt profound relief. It had been months since she'd been apart—with the exception of a few hours here and there—from Lenz Buchmann, and now, for the first time in ages, because of the various procedures that needed carrying out, she was going to spend two nights alone, away from home.

Apart from Gustav Liegnitz, Buchmann also had with him a nurse hired specifically for those two days. The seriousness of his illness meant he could no longer be without another person looking after him, and Gustav just wasn't made for particular tasks—like those, for instance, that involved practical acts of hygiene, which could be upsetting to certain temperaments. Lenz Buchmann no longer needed a man or a woman beside him, he needed only a nurse. In this respect, everything went according to plan: the nurse did her job.

But it was during these two days of Julia's absence that the aforementioned event took place, an event that might help to clarify a little—given this penchant for useless cruelty, from which he could draw no benefit—the character of Gustav Liegnitz. He was resentful, he flew into rages, got angry, used his strength when he came out stronger, tried to survive when he was the weaker party. That was Gustav.

On the first night of Julia's absence, with no real idea of how to justify the act, without even having planned it, the moment Buchmann fell asleep—Lenz now spent the best part of his days asleep—Gustav took the piece of paper on which Buchmann's father's name was written (a piece of paper that Lenz would read each night, muttering the name several times so as not to forget), and replaced it with another piece of paper on which he had written not a name but a phrase.

The truth was that, for two whole nights, Buchmann, no longer having any sense of reality and stripped of all his defense mechanisms, read Gustav's pathetic, shameful phrase—which assaulted his most intimate values, albeit in a childish way—without any consequences, and he read it—albeit with a sense of strangeness—convinced that he was reading and repeating the name of his father.

After this incident, perpetrated by Gustav Liegnitz, which nobody knew about, because the piece of paper was removed before Julia got back, Lenz Buchmann, now using the right piece of paper again, resumed—without surprise, as though nothing had happened, as though he had always been reading the same thing—the same desperate exercise of trying to hold in his head to the very end the name of his father, that most important man-at-arms: Frederich Taubert Buchmann.

Frederich Taubert Buchmann, Frederich Taubert Buchmann, repeated, tireless, labored, the dying Lenz—this was his final task.

A SURPRISE BEHIND HIS BACK

1

Stretching out and lengthening

Julia had already been back for several days when her brother, the deaf-mute Gustav, appeared in front of her, grinning, both his hands behind his back.

With his struggled *mmm*s he said—and Julia understood— something like, You want to see what I have behind my back?

Julia smiled. The atmosphere had been so tense lately that a little happiness like this, an explicit happiness, on her brother's face, was too good to waste. The thought that it might be a gift occurred to her, that her brother had for some reason wanted to reward her, had remembered her efforts to keep the house in order and, above all, to look after Buchmann.

Her brother, still smiling, brought his hands around from behind him and showed Julia a little mouse in a mousetrap, dead. Julia gave a little scream. The little gray mouse had come apart; it had been practically decapitated by the impact of the metal, and there were only a few threads, a few slender connections, keeping the mouse—so to speak—a single unit.

The rest of the body, meanwhile, not having been caught by the crushing part of the trap, had suffered, by extension, a serious shock, and though still in one piece—unlike the part that formerly connected the head to the rest of the mouse's body—seemed to have been simultaneously lengthened and shortened. It looked, in fact, as though this had been the cause of death: two opposed forces acting in a single place at the same time, and this single body unable to bear their simultaneous effects: a force that sought to shorten—perhaps this was what the mouse would have wanted? (or could this, the shortening, have been the mousetrap's idea?)— and then another that wanted to stretch out as much as possible.

Julia was horrified, but she didn't look away. To Julia's eyes, not used to the workings of a mousetrap, everything looked strange: could it have been the mouse that had tried to stretch out, to reach the food, or had it been the mousetrap that (like two men pulling in different directions) had forced its body to extend over an area greater than was tolerable to a living organism?

Gustav then murmured something like: I got it. And Julia, disgusted, insulted Gustav for having shown that thing to her.

And Gustav said, with his gestures, that he thought—because of the position and quantity of feces—that this had been the only mouse. And it had been hunted down.

FINAL EXAM

1

Looking for big things

Lenz's physical decline was irreparable, and the visits of the doctor who had been taking care of him from the beginning were by now purely symbolic.

Julia was present, however, for what might be called Lenz's final exam before death, conducted by Dr. Selig, one of the biggest names in medicine in those days—which just went to show the power and respect that even this decaying body possessed and imposed, even on the verge of the end.

To Julia this all seemed like a strange kind of autopsy, an autopsy conducted in the watchful presence of the dead man, a nonintrusive autopsy that only ran along the surface of the body, but which nonetheless retained —at least to her eyes—the appearance of exhaustiveness and rigor. Julia was present at all these procedures, beginning—which caused some surprise—on Dr. Buchmann's scalp.

It seemed to Julia that Dr. Selig was looking—absurdly—on Buchmann's dying body, for head-lice; as if head-lice (and their possible existence), thought Julia, had any importance at that moment. It also occurred to Julia that she should intervene and tell Dr. Selig that—great though the respect his erudition had earned him—it was now a question of looking for and resolving big problems; he should leave the little problems alone.

It became clear, however, that this was not the case, that Dr. Selig was not looking for head-lice on this passive Lenz Buchmann's scalp, but something quite different. Perhaps a particular coloring, a lack of hair that meant something—what did Julia know about medicine, after all? She ought merely to observe, observe and not say a word.

And Julia didn't say a word.

2
The child's little hammer

So Dr. Selig, as we have described, began at the scalp and then went over all the intermediate areas of the body, ending up at the soles of Lenz's bare feet. At each of the parts of Buchmann's body the doctor stopped, observed, analyzed, sometimes writing down a few words in his notepad. He also—when Buchmann was able to cooperate—did some little tests. On the soles of his feet, for example, he used a little hammer, which reminded Julia of a toy, reminded her of a child's toy, a child playing at building things. There was no playing here, though—exactly the opposite. The tone and atmosphere in the room were of an unyielding seriousness. Nobody smiled. The doctor didn't even—as was usual in these situations—make any little jokes to relieve the tension. He was a technician, that was clear, and he was no doubt very good on that objective level, though it was quite noticeable at that moment—Julia noticed it—that he was someone who still had something to learn. It was obvious that in the middle of those tests he was putting Buchmann through—*Talk a little just so I can hear how your voice is doing . . . now, can you move your legs, your toes?*—in the middle of this exam that seemed nothing more than a repeat of any basic first-year medical exam, that there, in the middle of all this tension, perhaps the doctor in charge ought to be able to show a little wit. At someone's deathbed, one ought to be able to maintain, as much as is possible, a relaxed atmosphere. After all, there was no longer anything to lose or to gain.

And that was the only thing really wrong in this examination, this final exam to which the dying Lenz Buchmann was subjected, carried out by Dr. Selig: the absence of any humor.

And why would a doctor bother with these kinds of tests? It seemed to Julia—she was wrong, surely—that this doctor was taking a certain pleasure in confirming with his little tests what any person, like her, without significant learning, just keeping her eyes open, could tell. Taking a morbid pleasure in confirming another man's weakness, a weakness that would never improve.

3

The weight borne by the hand (difficult questions)

One of the little tests that Dr. Selig did was to check how much weight Lenz's hands were still capable of supporting. Although it could not technically be classified as such, Lenz's left hand was really already dead; it no longer existed as a hand—a part of the body made to grip, pull, hold, push. Lenz's left hand didn't even have the strength to hold a piece of paper for a couple of seconds. And this, actually, was the test that Dr. Selig performed.

Why do this? was what Julia didn't stop thinking. It seemed to her a useless humiliation.

The aim was to find out for how many seconds Lenz's left hand could remain suspended over his mattress, in the air. The sheet of paper was important, not for its meager weight but as a decoy, a pretext for Lenz's hand to be raised. It was an attempt to give the test some meaning. That it was a pretext was clear from Dr. Selig's improvising a little; for it was only when he saw that Buchmann hadn't the least interest in raising his hand that the doctor proposed the idea that Lenz try to keep a piece of paper in the air for a few seconds.

It was he—the doctor—who, without asking permission, with an abruptness that in any other context would have been considered completely indelicate, grabbed the piece of paper that was right there, so nearby, on Mr. Buchmann's bedside table.

Of course it didn't matter what was written on it—and Julia, truth be told, didn't notice this (doubtless involuntary) invasion of Buchmann's privacy. She was thinking about other things, things very far away, and all that mattered for this test was the sheet of paper itself, the substance, the bait: to see how long Buchmann's hand was capable of remaining in the air.

But, in the end, Lenz's left hand didn't rise at all—through lack of strength (clearly), but also perhaps through lack of interest.

With his right hand, however, there was a different result. Lenz Buchmann was able to raise this hand a few centimeters—and Dr. Selig, immediately, helping him, put the dying man's fingers into a pincer-grip, so as to hold the sheet of paper with whatever strength he could.

"Try now," said Dr. Selig, "to keep your hand in the air as long as possible." But he hadn't even finished saying these words when the dying man's hand fell back onto the comfortable support of the mattress.

It was then that Julia took the piece of paper, and only then did she notice that it was the same sheet on which she had written the full name of Lenz's father: Frederich Buchmann. She didn't assign any significance to this detail, however. There was no time for that. Dr. Selig had already moved on from Buchmann's hands to his chest, to how well his lungs were working.

"Breathe in deeply," Dr. Selig was saying now—"and then, as hard as you can, exhale as much air as you can manage."

Dr. Selig asked Lenz to do this, and next to the bed, standing there, a few meters from this relentless examination, which seemed (as has been said) like something out of school, asking only basic questions but grading the answers with a neutral, inscrutable rigor, while this exam ran its course, Julia, like a good student whispering the answers to a weaker one, breathed in as deeply as she could and then breathed out, doing unconsciously—and in as restrained a manner as she could manage, though there was no reason for this—what Mr. Buchmann himself was no longer capable of doing.

PART THREE

DEATH

THE SUICIDE READIES HIMSELF

1
Like father, like son

Those small moments of consciousness he still had allowed Lenz Buchmann to make a decision. He spoke to Julia, as he could not help but do, and she, though shocked, did not react irrationally. She knew the state of, if not Lenz's health—it had been a long time since that word had been used in the house—then his illness, and she knew, too, of the reverence with which he held certain Buchmann family principles. It wasn't the first time the subject had been broached; Mr. Buchmann had also mentioned it earlier—in the days when Julia Liegnitz still carried out (with such evident professionalism) the duties of a secretary.

Lenz's father, Frederich, had killed himself with a gunshot to the head, and to the son—a Buchmann—the idea that it was his duty to die only by the force of metal was an *idée fixe*, nonnegotiable. But Lenz, at this point in his illness, now needed help to fulfill this obligation.

What had happened to bring him to this humiliating position? What had happened to him, that at this moment he understood quite clearly that he didn't have the strength—the objective, muscular, organic strength? How had he got things wrong, that he had reached the point of not being able to pick up a pistol and fire it at himself? How could he have reached a point where he couldn't—under his own power, with his own body—carry out this primal command? The truth was that for the young, eighteen-year-old Lenz, and then for the well-regarded doctor, just as, later, for the politician, there had never been any doubt. He had learned from his father Frederich's words, and then, later, from his practical example, that no true Buchmann could allow himself to die, gradually, from illness. Only an abrupt, violent death would be acceptable. By accident, at war, or through suicide. There was no other way to leave the room, to use Frederich's expression.

Moreover, the death by illness of his brother Albert had made it even clearer that a weak man dies in a weak way, and that he—Lenz Buchmann—was from different stock, was made of the same timber as Frederich, not at all like those people who make the most of what little they have left, dragging things out till the very last moment, subsisting on whatever few crumbs they're thrown.

And then, once more, he was the last of his branch of the Buchmanns. Therefore, he knew he must have made a mistake somewhere along the way. The image came to him of chickens pecking at the little crumbs someone is leaving them.

He—Lenz Buchmann—without being completely aware of the state he was in at the time, had been transformed into one of those insignificant animals who never give up, right until the last second, scraping away at their own existences until they have nothing, not a bit, left to give. And, in fact, his mistake had been precisely that: he hadn't recognized the moment when his illness had leaped over the fissure that separated the two shores by such a distance that no human leap could now transport him back to the other side. It had been a long time now since Lenz had lost the strength to return, but he hadn't realized this. Until now he had been convinced that he would recover. Sometimes, even in recent days, during his short moments of access to lucid consciousness, to his old consciousness, he saw himself recovering the place that was due to him, thanks to the manifest will of the people: the position of vice president of the Party. And he found himself carrying out strategic maneuvers—he was still imagining where he ought to place the bomb that would kill president Hamm Kestner.

This, then, had been his mistake: the false sense that he could still accomplish things, that *this* was not over yet.

But the truth was, there was no going back.

And it was on one of the days following Dr. Selig's rigorous examination that Buchmann asked Julia to help him to die. He wasn't—he'd finally seen this for certain during the exam to which he'd been subjected—capable of picking up a weapon. He no longer had the strength. The only thing he asked was that she hold the weapon for him, he would squeeze the trigger himself. That was his responsibility—he didn't want to pass it on to her, this last weight.

2

If it's not me, it's you

As we've already said, knowing all about Buchmann's past, his ideas, and his almost inhuman connection to the figure of his father, and to his father's example, it was obvious to Julia that this was a request that could not be refused. Refusing it wouldn't be fair.

For Julia it was the most important task that Dr. Buchmann had ever put—now, literally—into her hands. She saw this final act as a task in which, just as in her other duties, she could not show any incompetence or hesitation.

Julia explained to Lenz, however, that she didn't think she would be able to go through with it.

During the next day, Julia thought of a solution. She spoke to Buchmann, then she spoke to her brother Gustav.

Then she spoke again to Mr. Buchmann alone. He agreed.

JULIA WANDERS THE CITY

1

Whatever could be happening in the Buchmann house?

That morning, Julia went out early. It was what had been arranged. She couldn't stay in the house.

As she closed the outer gate she looked back toward the main façade. There, albeit with its black color quite faded, was the phrase: *Death to Lenz Buchmann!*

It was a similar situation all over the city. The various *Death to Lenz Buchmann!* phrases had disappeared entirely, bit by bit, or at least been diluted by the elements, especially the sun. At the most important sites—public places, the Party headquarters, the walls of the hospitals and the fire department—in those places of significance, the phrase had been immediately eliminated: painted over. But really, although it was covered, the phrase still seemed to be there, to some people—still seemed to be in those places it had been seen. The phrase was hidden now, yes, but it was as though an energy were being emitted from whatever part of the hospital wall or wall of the Party headquarters it had once been seen—an energy like that which emerges from the ground where you know a body is buried. Sometimes a father passing by one of these walls would tell his son (pointing over to an innocuous, clean wall, all a solid color): here's one of the places where they wrote *Death to Lenz Buchmann!*

The public places, then, were the ones that, in spite of everything, forgot most quickly, so to speak, the phrase that someone had once written in them. In other places, far less important places— some private house or other, for example—the last traces of the phrase were far more apparent, as less organized or even careless people had simply gone over the words with one more coat of paint, leaving it at that, like a muffled shout from the bottom of a well: *Death to Lenz Buchmann!*

There was even one private house whose owner had been away for many years, living abroad, and so the inscription remained intact. It's important to stress that among all the places that the deaf-mute Gustav—on that one night, sneaking around—had marked with that phrase, his work always remained and resisted best in those secondary places that Gustav had chosen randomly, by instinct or chance, for his targets. Whereas, looking at the list of places that Lenz Buchmann had ordered Gustav to mark with the phrase, and of which he'd insisted—to Gustav—that these were the sites where it would be most important, it was in these supposedly most significant places that the phrase had been comprehensively erased, and so almost forgotten.

Julia, who only learned the origin of the phrase much later, had been just as surprised as the rest of the city on the morning when it first appeared. Even frightened. Someone, she thought then, wanted Lenz Buchmann dead, and perhaps was even planning such a thing.

Throughout the city, and the various organisms inhabiting it, the appearance of the phrase had also prompted—of course—a number of processes of enquiry. But nobody was arrested, in the end, and nothing was objectively proved against anyone. At the time no one even mentioned Gustav.

In any case, on this particular morning, Julia had more to think about than those turbulent weeks when the name of Lenz Buchmann—in reality already a very sick man—had again, strange though it seemed, returned to dominate the city. Like a ghost, some had said.

2

Has something already happened?

Even while she is looking at the phrase *Death to Lenz Buchmann!*, almost completely faded on the main façade of Lenz's house (it had never been removed, at the express wish of Dr. Buchmann: *I don't want people ever to forget I was threatened*), Julia is already thinking about something else.

At that moment she's imagining what might be happening in the house. And as she makes her way further into the city her heart begins to beat faster. As each minute passes, the probability that something is happening, or has already happened, increases. Julia doesn't stop thinking about this.

She feels a certain regret, too, about not being there for the final moment of Lenz Buchmann's life, but she also thinks—she can't help thinking—about some plans she's made, about what she still has to change in the house, what she should do with that room, after so many months of it being imbued with illness. How to clean it . . .

As she advances at a slow pace—she is wandering in order to be seen, she stops at shops, asks the occasional question, buys something, goes back out onto the street, is seen, sees—she is also thinking about the details of Lenz's funeral.

They had talked about this occasionally, and, yes, he wanted a lot of people present, the whole city around him, as though he was the man in the center again, the man where orders came from, the big decisions. He was sure—he had said this, explicitly, to Julia— that the fact of his having died from a bullet to the head, tragically, abruptly, thus refusing to accept the progressive nature of the illness, he was sure that this gesture *would get people really fired up*, that had been the expression he'd used; the suicide would make his funeral more popular than ever.

He knew exactly what was going to happen. The Church, eager not to miss out on such an important moment, would pretend that there had been no suicide, but a simple death demanded by nature, and hence would participate with great pomp in Lenz's funeral. Yet, throughout the city, in the newspapers for example, the act would be quite clear—albeit perhaps in some articles the cause of death might be stated in such a way as to remain ambiguous; suicide was always shocking, and the newspapers showed a sort of modesty about putting the fact of someone's killing themselves into black and white, especially if the person had been in ill health.

In any case, one way or other, whether clearly or ambiguously, from talk on the streets or via some other route, people would learn that Lenz Buchmann had committed suicide—and with that gesture, Lenz was quite sure, he would win over everyone's subservient minds, one last time. It was as though, once dead, people would still be coming to ask him for favors—or that was his ambition.

There Julia is, in the middle of the city, thinking about these things and showing herself—exhibiting herself—thanks to an instinct that was hardly noble but which she couldn't control: *You see? I'm right here while everything's happening.*

There's nothing linking me to Buchmann's suicide, that's what Julia is really saying when, for the tenth time, she repeats a pleasant but restrained greeting to an acquaintance she passes.

3

The importance of a finger

At Lenz Buchmann's house—which in truth had long been Julia Liegnitz's house—the man who bore the same name as his father, Gustav Liegnitz, goes into the dying man's bedroom. Lenz, his eyes open, receives him with a grimace that is vaguely reminiscent of a smile, and is indeed an attempt at one.

In a sense, Buchmann is still trying to run things. He is the one in charge, the one with control of the situation in his hands—that's what he tries to convey with his look and with the minimal gestures he is still able to make. With a slight movement of the index finger of his right hand, he points at the drawer, but this is meaningless, as Gustav knows very well where the pistol is; that finger is only an attempt to remain in charge, to remain at the center.

Gustav takes the pistol from the drawer.

Even more slowly than his illness requires, so that that deaf-mute will understand him (where did that deaf-mute come from, who is he? Lenz doesn't recall, though his mind retains the idea that the deaf-mute is here to do *that*), Lenz asks that he hold the weapon for him, only that.

Gustav, the deaf-mute, does as they agreed: he takes Buchmann's right hand, a hand that is so light as to feel completely weightless, and bends and guides its fingers so that they wrap around the grip of the pistol.

Dr. Buchmann has his whole hand—all his fingers—on the grip, with no strength at all: it is Gustav who keeps his hand from falling.

Then the deaf-mute, one of his hands stopping Lenz's from falling, uses his other to put the index finger of that passive, empty hand in front of the trigger. Gustav Liegnitz puts Buchmann's index finger in the right position.

Still holding that docile hand, he now directs it, both the hand and the weapon that the pliable hand is already allowing to droop too low, he directs it in such a way that, at last, Buchmann's hand has the barrel of the weapon pointing at his own head.

Gustav is only—with the greatest care—holding on to Buchmann's hand so that it doesn't waver.

It is possible to see that, on the trigger, Lenz Buchmann's index finger is trying to do something. The deaf-mute sees it quite clearly, a few small movements, the finger contracting slightly. But it's not enough.

What is needed is for the finger to contract, to bend, and then, continuing this movement, to push the trigger back. That's what is needed, Gustav seems to be thinking, or the bullet won't come out.

Now the deaf-mute notices the expression on Dr. Lenz Buchmann's face. A face that barely exists any longer, that no longer has flesh; it's struggling, is making a truly super-human effort, far more than human, it is conspicuous and Gustav sees it. All the strength left in Buchmann is concentrated not only on this situation but specifically in that finger, in that one finger. Even the rest of the hand doesn't matter anymore.

Buchmann has already realized that the deaf-mute is holding firm and won't let his hand drop. More than that—the firmness of the deaf-mute is such that Buchmann's hand almost doesn't shake. The rest, however, is up to him. It is up to that one finger, that index finger. Everything is waiting for him, for that finger, and Lenz—and his face, which had long been inexpressive, now, suddenly anguished, shows everything—is trying everything, concentrating all his energy in that single finger.

And the finger does indeed move again, now more noticeably. He pushes the trigger, but it isn't really a push, it's more of a touch. More strength is needed, Dr. Buchmann, more strength.

Lenz Buchmann makes yet another, final attempt, but with even less obvious results than in the previous instance. Even on that tiny scale, he has gone past a certain point: he is already losing his strength; it is irreversible.

It's then that Lenz asks Gustav explicitly to fire; he can't manage it on his own. The deaf-mute should squeeze the trigger. This is what Buchmann asks, speaking with great difficulty because of his exhaustion. The deaf-mute doesn't understand the actual words being spoken, but it's easy enough to understand what it is that Buchmann wants. On first impulse, Gustav's right hand does move, but stops very far—far on this scale, anyway—from arriving at where the trigger is.

Gustav's two hands then react at just the same moment, almost instinctually, it seems, and with scorn and even disgust they abandon the task in which his energies had been engaged. Without this support from Gustav's hands, Buchmann's right hand immediately falls, and thus, almost simultaneously, three things happen: the deaf-mute pulls his hands away from it all; Buchmann's arm falls loosely, half on the mattress and half off; and the weapon immediately drops, making a little noise on the floor of the room, an unexpected and inoffensive thud.

ONE LAST ATTEMPT FOR THE WORD TO BE HEARD

1

Solidity and resistance

Lenz wasn't far from being the age his brother Albert had died at, but how could he remember that now?

Lenz Buchmann continued—day after day, at a frightening, galloping pace—to lose his memory. However, no sooner had the man entered—with that delicate, formal dragging of feet with which one makes one's way into the sickroom of a dying man—than Buchmann had the immediate feeling that he recognized him. Let us say that, in order not to frighten Lenz (at Julia's suggestion? that much is unknown), the man presented himself without what we might call his "moral equipment." He was dressed like a civilian, and there was nothing about him that gave him away, apart from (but perhaps this was plenty) the cross he wore on top of his clothes.

He was not, however, attempting to hide why he had come; he only wanted to keep from giving Lenz too much of a shock to begin with; going in softly, in street clothes and not the clothes of someone who is going to try and extract from a dying man a final benevolent hope. But as we have said, Lenz recognized him at once.

From where? Who was he?

After that came the calm words, but they only served to calm the man himself, because Lenz was thinking about something else.

The words, meanwhile, kept on coming and coming, one after another, making up a speech that Buchmann also began to recognize, seemingly reminiscent of a forgotten childhood song, a song whose melody is recalled many years later.

He was a priest, and he was there to give Lenz his last rites—the situation was now clear to Lenz.

But which priest was he? Hadn't they, the two of them, met before in some other situation? Buchmann, with one of his sudden accesses of memory, which were increasingly rare, remembered clearly the conversation he had had with a priest inside a church; the way he had frightened the priest, and the way he had felt the fear in him. Was this the same one? Or not? How could he know? To Lenz they were all the same. How could he—in the situation in which he found himself—remember the face of someone he had then considered entirely unimportant? How could he remember another face that had been afraid of him?

He did remember—yes, and quite clearly, too—the faces of the two or three men who at certain points of his life had made *him* afraid: a primary-school teacher, he remembered him very well; and the madman Rafa—now his face came very clearly to Lenz's mind. He had been afraid of the madman; at last he'd understood that.

Yes, those faces he remembered well. But how to remember the hundreds of faces whom—on the contrary—he, Lenz Buchmann, had frightened?

In any case, he knew that whether or not this was the same priest, the man was doubtless here to take his revenge for having been defeated in the past.

The priest was already well into his process, immersed in an uninterrupted speech, a speech so solid that it seemed to be made up of just a single word. There he was, frightening Lenz; bringing up, here and there, words like *heaven*, *hell*, and a few times, several times, the word *devil*.

2

Please, come closer

While the priest was still speaking, all Buchmann could think about was the moment when he would be alone with Julia and could insult her for this stupid audacity of hers, for this extra step she had taken without his authorization. At that moment, however, the most urgent thing to be resolved was right there, little more than a meter and a half from Lenz's tired head: that grotesque face, both hypnotized and trying to hypnotize. *A hypnotized man trying to hypnotize*, thought Lenz, clearly, about the priest.

This was a madman he had to get rid of quickly, as he couldn't bear the sound of those words, that repetition, that insistence, that force that had no more than one or two arguments and that repeated them exhaustively; going down one road, then the other. Trying—so it seemed to Lenz—to find the one weak part of his body that would say, even if only out of exhaustion, Yes, thrice yes.

Buchmann, however, not really knowing what it was the priest was saying at that moment—he seemed to have the longest word in the world in his mouth—no longer hearing him at all, was thinking about saying *No, No* out loud. He immediately felt, however, that the effort would be pointless. He wouldn't be able to do it. Which was why he did something else. With a little gesture he let the priest—who was already almost on top of him—understand that he wanted him to come even closer.

3

Losing on one side, winning on the other

Lenz made the signal, and the priest, being helpful, immediately brought his face closer to Lenz's, getting ready to turn his neck slightly so that he could hear what Lenz apparently wanted to whisper in his ear. But before this little turning of his neck, Lenz, gathering all his strength at that moment into his mouth, was already making progress spitting—a wad of saliva that he first felt come together and then leave his mouth, or at least try to leave his mouth, since because of his weakness and the position his neck was in (the nape of his neck completely against the mattress) what actually happened was that his spittle was never projected, and what seemed inside his mouth to be a firm wad to be spat into the eyes of the priest had, from the outside, from outside that body, been seen as an involuntary carelessness, a loss of control, which left his face—Lenz Buchmann's face—smeared with his own saliva, immediately above and below his lips and on his chin. Only a single droplet, almost insubstantial, had reached the face of the priest. Immediately, as she was in the habit of doing, Julia wiped the saliva from the corner of Lenz's mouth and his chin.

Minutes later the priest left Dr. Lenz Buchmann's room, re-spectfully—even before he was out the door—making the sign of the cross.

The new lady of the house, Julia Liegnitz, then said good-bye at the door, very cordially, even though both she and the priest showed their sadness at the irreversible condition of the sick man and his lack of interest in the priest's words and this last attempt at reconversion. Neither the priest nor Julia had sensed even the slightest hostility on Buchmann's part in relation to that visit. The insulting attempt to spit right into the eyes of this representative of the Church had only happened inside Dr. Buchmann's head, and inside his body; the same Dr. Buchmann who by now—the will in which he left all his property to Julia Liegnitz had been definitively validated days earlier—was merely the former owner of the house.

The new house, that house, Julia Liegnitz's, and she herself as its owner—following an old Liegnitz tradition—kept their eyes turned respectfully toward the Church. The Church had a new conquest there, and in spite of the apparent failure of his attempt to reclaim Lenz, the priest's satisfaction when he said good-bye to Julia and to Gustav—who had in the meantime appeared—was more than visible.

EPILOGUE

1
The light

Occasionally Lenz Buchmann closes his eyes, but opens them again right away. The whole surface of his body is resting comfortably on the mattress. Only his head is slightly raised, on a pillow. This position of his head allows him, though lying down, to look at the television.

The truth is, Lenz Buchmann no longer sees the images. What happens, what is happening in that piece of equipment, the actual content, is something he can no longer comprehend, neither on a mental level nor visually. Images might appear of a tragic flood or of a children's game and he wouldn't be able to distinguish between the two events.

What he sees at that moment is merely a succession of bursts of light, bursts that seem to be coming toward him. He sees the light appearing, then disappearing again, and reappearing. He also sees that the light doesn't always stay the same color: that it is sometimes darker, other times blue, other times lighter.

It's strange, that light, and doesn't seem to belong to the same family as the light from the electric lamp. It's a completely different light. What seems to be happening in that television set, he thinks, is a malfunction: something has broken and it's no longer possible to see the world, only a beam of light turning on and turning off.

It occurs to him to call someone to fix it, this broken machine. I can't see anything anymore! he would shout then, if he still had the strength. But he does not. And he actually likes what's happening: there's a quite uncommon calmness coming out of that television set. No sound, and anyway, he's so focused on its light that if someone shouted from inside the house he wouldn't hear it. And now there are just his eyes. Only they have stayed behind, constituting his final resistance, the final barrier.

Lenz Buchmann was totally immobile and only his eyes, now and again, blinked. The light that came from the television set was undeniably a bright light, but the pleasure it gave Lenz just kept growing. He had never felt like this before: comfortable, protected: under that beam of light, nothing could happen to him.

He had been waiting for this for a long time, he thought, and it occurred to him that soon it would be good to ask them to fill the whole room with television sets.

That would have been the moment he would have wanted to call for someone, but he couldn't remember a single name to call.

The different tones of light followed one another, but within that variation, their agitated appearance, Buchmann had found—had located with his eyes—a constant line, another luminosity of the screen that remained independent of the movement of the light closer to the surface.

Lenz Buchmann understood, then, that the shafts of light, while they were calming him, were calling him by name at the same time.

Resting on the mattress, his hands brought him lightness, a weightlessness—he was freed from the burden of having to hang on to things, and his fingers, each one of them, seemed to be feeling this freedom, and, with utter serenity, they waited. The rest of his body didn't exist. At least, he didn't feel it. It had disappeared.

He was, then, just there: Lenz Buchmann, left behind, alone, with his eyes.

The light—that light didn't stop calling him. He wanted to feel hatred, but he couldn't. It calmed him, and called him. ·

Then there was, perhaps, a pause, and again a bright light came from the television that called him by his name. And now he went; he let himself go.

From the notebooks of Gonçalo M. Tavares | 23

GONÇALO M. TAVARES was born in 1970. He has published numerous books since 2001 and has been awarded an impressive number of literary prizes in a very short time, including the Saramago Prize in 2005.

DANIEL HAHN is a writer, an editor, and a translator from Spanish, Portuguese, and French. He has translated nine novels (winning the 2007 Independent Foreign Fiction Prize for *The Book of Chameleons* by José Eduardo Agualusa), as well as works of nonfiction by writers ranging from Portuguese Nobel laureate José Saramago to Brazilian footballer Pelé.

SELECTED DALKEY ARCHIVE PAPERBACKS

CARLOS FUENTES, *Christopher Unborn.*
  Distant Relations.
  Terra Nostra.
  Where the Air Is Clear.
JANICE GALLOWAY, *Foreign Parts.*
  The Trick Is to Keep Breathing.
WILLIAM H. GASS, *Cartesian Sonata
    and Other Novellas.*
  Finding a Form.
  A Temple of Texts.
  The Tunnel.
  Willie Masters' Lonesome Wife.
GÉRARD GAVARRY, *Hoppla! 1 2 3.*
  Making a Novel.
ETIENNE GILSON,
  The Arts of the Beautiful.
  Forms and Substances in the Arts.
C. S. GISCOMBE, *Giscome Road.*
  Here.
  Prairie Style.
DOUGLAS GLOVER, *Bad News of the Heart.*
  The Enamoured Knight.
WITOLD GOMBROWICZ,
  A Kind of Testament.
KAREN ELIZABETH GORDON,
  The Red Shoes.
GEORGI GOSPODINOV, *Natural Novel.*
JUAN GOYTISOLO, *Count Julian.*
  Exiled from Almost Everywhere.
  Juan the Landless.
  Makbara.
  Marks of Identity.
PATRICK GRAINVILLE, *The Cave of Heaven.*
HENRY GREEN, *Back.*
  Blindness.
  Concluding.
  Doting.
  Nothing.
JIŘÍ GRUŠA, *The Questionnaire.*
GABRIEL GUDDING,
  Rhode Island Notebook.
MELA HARTWIG, *Am I a Redundant
    Human Being?*
JOHN HAWKES, *The Passion Artist.*
  Whistlejacket.
ALEKSANDAR HEMON, ED.,
  Best European Fiction.
AIDAN HIGGINS, *A Bestiary.*
  Balcony of Europe.
  Bornholm Night-Ferry.
  Darkling Plain: Texts for the Air.
  Flotsam and Jetsam.
  Langrishe, Go Down.
  Scenes from a Receding Past.
  Windy Arbours.
KEIZO HINO, *Isle of Dreams.*
KAZUSHI HOSAKA, *Plainsong.*
ALDOUS HUXLEY, *Antic Hay.*
  Crome Yellow.
  Point Counter Point.
  Those Barren Leaves.
  Time Must Have a Stop.
NAOYUKI II, *The Shadow of a Blue Cat.*
MIKHAIL IOSSEL AND JEFF PARKER, EDS.,
  *Amerika: Russian Writers View the
    United States.*
GERT JONKE, *The Distant Sound.*
  Geometric Regional Novel.
  Homage to Czerny.
  The System of Vienna.

JACQUES JOUET, *Mountain R.*
  Savage.
  Upstaged.
CHARLES JULIET, *Conversations with
    Samuel Beckett and Bram van
    Velde.*
MIEKO KANAI, *The Word Book.*
YORAM KANIUK, *Life on Sandpaper.*
HUGH KENNER, *The Counterfeiters.*
  *Flaubert, Joyce and Beckett:
    The Stoic Comedians.*
  Joyce's Voices.
DANILO KIŠ, *Garden, Ashes.*
  A Tomb for Boris Davidovich.
ANITA KONKKA, *A Fool's Paradise.*
GEORGE KONRÁD, *The City Builder.*
TADEUSZ KONWICKI, *A Minor Apocalypse.*
  The Polish Complex.
MENIS KOUMANDAREAS, *Koula.*
ELAINE KRAF, *The Princess of 72nd Street.*
JIM KRUSOE, *Iceland.*
EWA KURYLUK, *Century 21.*
EMILIO LASCANO TEGUI, *On Elegance
    While Sleeping.*
ERIC LAURRENT, *Do Not Touch.*
HERVÉ LE TELLIER, *The Sextine Chapel.*
  *A Thousand Pearls (for a Thousand
    Pennies)*
VIOLETTE LEDUC, *La Bâtarde.*
EDOUARD LEVÉ, *Suicide.*
SUZANNE JILL LEVINE, *The Subversive
    Scribe: Translating Latin
    American Fiction.*
DEBORAH LEVY, *Billy and Girl.*
  *Pillow Talk in Europe and Other
    Places.*
JOSÉ LEZAMA LIMA, *Paradiso.*
ROSA LIKSOM, *Dark Paradise.*
OSMAN LINS, *Avalovara.*
  The Queen of the Prisons of Greece.
ALF MAC LOCHLAINN,
  The Corpus in the Library.
  Out of Focus.
RON LOEWINSOHN, *Magnetic Field(s).*
MINA LOY, *Stories and Essays of Mina Loy.*
BRIAN LYNCH, *The Winner of Sorrow.*
D. KEITH MANO, *Take Five.*
MICHELINE AHARONIAN MARCOM,
  The Mirror in the Well.
BEN MARCUS,
  The Age of Wire and String.
WALLACE MARKFIELD,
  Teitlebaum's Window.
  To an Early Grave.
DAVID MARKSON, *Reader's Block.*
  Springer's Progress.
  Wittgenstein's Mistress.
CAROLE MASO, *AVA.*
LADISLAV MATEJKA AND KRYSTYNA
  POMORSKA, EDS.,
  *Readings in Russian Poetics:
    Formalist and Structuralist Views.*
HARRY MATHEWS,
  *The Case of the Persevering Maltese:
    Collected Essays.*
  Cigarettes.
  The Conversions.
  *The Human Country: New and
    Collected Stories.*
  The Journalist.

My Life in CIA.
Singular Pleasures.
The Sinking of the Odradek Stadium.
Tlooth.
20 Lines a Day.
JOSEPH MCELROY,
Night Soul and Other Stories.
THOMAS MCGONIGLE,
Going to Patchogue.
ROBERT L. MCLAUGHLIN, ED., *Innovations: An Anthology of Modern & Contemporary Fiction.*
ABDELWAHAB MEDDEB, *Talismano.*
HERMAN MELVILLE, *The Confidence-Man.*
AMANDA MICHALOPOULOU, *I'd Like.*
STEVEN MILLHAUSER,
The Barnum Museum.
In the Penny Arcade.
RALPH J. MILLS, JR.,
Essays on Poetry.
MOMUS, *The Book of Jokes.*
CHRISTINE MONTALBETTI, *Western.*
OLIVE MOORE, *Spleen.*
NICHOLAS MOSLEY, *Accident.*
Assassins.
Catastrophe Practice.
Children of Darkness and Light.
Experience and Religion.
God's Hazard.
The Hesperides Tree.
Hopeful Monsters.
Imago Bird.
Impossible Object.
Inventing God.
Judith.
Look at the Dark.
Natalie Natalia.
Paradoxes of Peace.
Serpent.
Time at War.
The Uses of Slime Mould: Essays of Four Decades.
WARREN MOTTE,
Fables of the Novel: French Fiction since 1990.
Fiction Now: The French Novel in the 21st Century.
Oulipo: A Primer of Potential Literature.
YVES NAVARRE, *Our Share of Time.*
Sweet Tooth.
DOROTHY NELSON, *In Night's City.*
Tar and Feathers.
ESHKOL NEVO, *Homesick.*
WILFRIDO D. NOLLEDO, *But for the Lovers.*
FLANN O'BRIEN,
At Swim-Two-Birds.
At War.
The Best of Myles.
The Dalkey Archive.
Further Cuttings.
The Hard Life.
The Poor Mouth.
The Third Policeman.
CLAUDE OLLIER, *The Mise-en-Scène.*
Wert and the Life Without End.
PATRIK OUŘEDNÍK, *Europeana.*
The Opportune Moment, 1855.
BORIS PAHOR, *Necropolis.*

FERNANDO DEL PASO,
News from the Empire.
Palinuro of Mexico.
ROBERT PINGET, *The Inquisitory.*
Mahu or The Material.
Trio.
MANUEL PUIG,
Betrayed by Rita Hayworth.
The Buenos Aires Affair.
Heartbreak Tango.
RAYMOND QUENEAU, *The Last Days.*
Odile.
Pierrot Mon Ami.
Saint Glinglin.
ANN QUIN, *Berg.*
Passages.
Three.
Tripticks.
ISHMAEL REED,
The Free-Lance Pallbearers.
The Last Days of Louisiana Red.
Ishmael Reed: The Plays.
Juice!
Reckless Eyeballing.
The Terrible Threes.
The Terrible Twos.
Yellow Back Radio Broke-Down.
JOÃO UBALDO RIBEIRO, *House of the Fortunate Buddhas.*
JEAN RICARDOU, *Place Names.*
RAINER MARIA RILKE, *The Notebooks of Malte Laurids Brigge.*
JULIÁN RÍOS, *The House of Ulysses.*
Larva: A Midsummer Night's Babel.
Poundemonium.
Procession of Shadows.
AUGUSTO ROA BASTOS, *I the Supreme.*
DANIËL ROBBERECHTS,
Arriving in Avignon.
JEAN ROLIN, *The Explosion of the Radiator Hose.*
OLIVIER ROLIN, *Hotel Crystal.*
ALIX CLEO ROUBAUD, *Alix's Journal.*
JACQUES ROUBAUD, *The Form of a City Changes Faster, Alas, Than the Human Heart.*
The Great Fire of London.
Hortense in Exile.
Hortense Is Abducted.
The Loop.
The Plurality of Worlds of Lewis.
The Princess Hoppy.
Some Thing Black.
LEON S. ROUDIEZ, *French Fiction Revisited.*
RAYMOND ROUSSEL, *Impressions of Africa.*
VEDRANA RUDAN, *Night.*
STIG SÆTERBAKKEN, *Siamese.*
LYDIE SALVAYRE, *The Company of Ghosts.*
Everyday Life.
The Lecture.
Portrait of the Writer as a Domesticated Animal.
The Power of Flies.
LUIS RAFAEL SÁNCHEZ,
Macho Camacho's Beat.
SEVERO SARDUY, *Cobra & Maitreya.*
NATHALIE SARRAUTE,
Do You Hear Them?
Martereau.
The Planetarium.